HUNTED BY THE DRAGON

CAPTURED BY A DRAGON-SHIFTER: A QURILIXEN WORLD SHORT NOVEL

MICHELLE M. PILLOW

MICHELLE M. PILLOW® - MICHELLEPILLOW.COM

ABOUT HUNTED BY THE DRAGON

Welcome to the dangerous world of Qurilixen where dragon-shifters and cat-shifters rule as fiercely as they love.

Bounty hunter by trade, dragon-shifter by birth, Seanan came to Earth in search of a mate. Two years later, he finds himself crossing paths with a woman he suspects may be exactly what he's been looking for--too bad the frustrating female is the reason he's stranded on Earth in the first place.

Qurilixen World Novels

Dragon Lords Series
Barbarian Prince
Perfect Prince
Dark Prince
Warrior Prince
His Highness The Duke
The Stubborn Lord
The Reluctant Lord
The Impatient Lord
The Dragon's Queen

Lords of the Var® Series
The Savage King
The Playful Prince
The Bound Prince
The Rogue Prince
The Pirate Prince

Captured by a Dragon-Shifter Series
Determined Prince
Rebellious Prince
Stranded with the Cajun
Hunted by the Dragon
Mischievous Prince
Headstrong Prince

Space Lords Series
His Frost Maiden
His Fire Maiden
His Metal Maiden
His Earth Maiden

His Woodland Maiden

Dynasty Lords Series
Seduction of the Phoenix
Temptation of the Butterfly

To learn more about the Qurilixen World series of
books and to stay up to date on the latest book list
visit www.MichellePillow.com

IF YOU'RE new to my books, the *Dragon Lords* are my bestselling futuristic shape-shifter romance series. The stories became reader favorites, and so I wrote things from their enemy's point of view in a spin-off series for the cat-shifting *Lords of the Var®*. Then they ventured off into the stars in the series installment *Space Lords*. Now, I'm time traveling with them back to our time with the series *Captured by a Dragon-Shifter*, which you are now reading book one of. Don't worry, I have the series reading order on my website to help you figure it all out, http://michellepillow.com/.

To those of you *not* new to my books, readers have emailed asking Dragon Lords cultural questions since the first dragon-shifting prince released years ago. I have teased you with a lot of little hints of how the Draig found brides in "the old days". Many of you have expressed wanting to climb aboard the space ship and sail away into the future—which would probably take some cryogenic freezing and a lot of icy waiting. Well, before you start packing those sweaters... I don't want any of you going to that extreme, so I've brought your favorite dragon-shifters and cat-shifters to modern-day Earth. They don't live on our planet, but they have recently started to revisit.

For *Dragon Lords* and *Lords of the Var*® fans, *Captured by a Dragon-Shifter* is a modern-day prequel series to those first books. They take place long before the princes you know and love ever found their mates, long before *The Dragon's Queen*, in a time when the dragon-shifters and cat-shifters actually—wait for it—*liked* each other and hung out as friends. They also don't have Galaxy Brides to bring them women. There's no one left to marry on the planet and things are starting to get desperate.

AUTHOR RECOMMENDS READING series installments in order of release for the simple fact she likes hiding little tidbits in the books as she goes and it's more fun that way, though each book can be read as a standalone if you prefer.

1

Draig Northern Mountains, Planet of Qurilixen

"Seanan, you don't have to do this." Galen fisted his hands and tapped them together in agitation. He appeared as if he wanted to brawl but had no outlet to take his frustrations out on. "Let someone else go."

The planet of Qurilixen's night of darkness cast shadows over the land, pierced only by the orange of firelight and the glow of stars. This was the one time a year the planet's three suns all set at the same time and, like most dragon-shifters, the brothers enjoyed spending this night outdoors. Earlier, they had shifted into dragon form and ran the valleys. Now, they rested by the fire.

"You have heard what our elders say about Earth," Galen insisted. "It is a horrible place that our people barely escaped. Humans are evil creatures by nature. Even the Reticulans won't land there, and those crazy aliens will be friends with anyone."

Seanan of the Draig forgave his younger brother's fear because it reflected his own. Only a fool wouldn't feel apprehension at the idea of being one of the first in centuries to go through a magical portal to another planet. But what choice did he have? "King Severin asked and it is my duty to go. It will be a quick journey. We will be through and back within moments. I promise you will see me again."

"It is easy for the Draig king to ask," Galen grumbled. "You do not hear his sons volunteering to go. Or the cat-shifter princes, for that matter. I don't see the Var king offering up any of his people for this mission."

"I don't think King Severin offered to let the cat-shifters come with us. The portal is on dragon land. It is right that we take charge of it. Cats are too wild, and though they are allies, I'm not sure they can be trusted with such a delicate matter."

"You know why King Severin asked you."

"Careful with your words, Galen. You are young but do not be foolish. Our rulers could be much worse than they are. Count that as a blessing."

"I am over a hundred years, and I speak the

truth," Galen answered. "He asked you because you only have me. With our parents dead, there will be I alone to protest your disappearance."

"That is why I go. If we don't find a steady supply of women our people will die, and there will be no one to protest it." Seanan closed his eyes and took a deep breath. "Without mates, we might as well lay down and die in this very spot, under these stars. Unless you've changed your mind and suddenly have feelings for Roswell the Reticulan?"

Galen laughed despite himself. The little gray alien man was hardly any dragon's type. In fact, the few alien races that had visited their planet were not wife material. Female humans were the only source they could come up with.

Shifter men thrived on Qurilixen, living longer and healthier than any other time in their history. Unfortunately, whatever caused shifter men to prosper was also killing their ability to produce female children. Most families had several sons in a misguided attempt to fight fate. Now, they had a generation full of mate-less males.

"Until we find a better solution, this is our path," Seanan said. "And when I am successful, we will be two of the first allowed to find mates as my reward. Think of it, a wife, children, love."

"I feel the loneliness, too. That is why I cannot lose the one family I have. Let me go with you tonight. If you are to meet death, I will meet it by your side." Galen stood as if he planned on marching until he reached the portal entrance.

Seanan was instantly on his feet. He grabbed his brother's arm tightly. His eyes shifted with the yellow warning of the dragon. "Stop this. I will see you again."

"What if the humans are standing guard on their side, waiting for us to come back? What if you land in a pit of spears? You know humans are waiting for our return. It only makes sense. Their leaders tried to massacre all shifters. They hate us. Even if you do manage to return with women, what kind of life will that be if they fear us?"

"The portal will not be open very long, as to lessen our chances of encountering problems. If we meet hostile enemies, our orders are to fight them and try to bring at least one back as a prisoner." Seanan took a deep breath and gazed up at the stars. He wondered what Earth would look like. The elders described castles surrounded by clusters of people ruled by angry zealots who tried to kill anyone who wasn't a pure human. That is why the dragon-shifters and cat-shifters escaped to a new world.

"I wish to find a wife as much as the next shifter, but this risks too much." Galen shook his head in denial. "No. This is wrong. The elders closed the portals for a reason. Humans hate us. They hunted us to near extinction and drove us from our homes. The elders blocked the portal cave so they could not follow us. Perhaps humans have done the same on their end."

"We sent a sphere on a chain through and brought it back several times. I do not believe the way is stoned over." Seanan did not want this moment to be filled with fighting. He had to trust his gods would lead him down the right path. "Wish me well, brother. The decision has been made."

"It would be something to have babies," Galen admitted, "and a woman."

"Keep that thought in mind and do not worry about me." Seanan grinned. "I promise we will see each other again. I know it in my heart. Tonight's trip is a simple task. There and back."

THERE AND BACK. A simple task. Do not worry. We will see each other again.

The unintentional arrogance of those statements

filled Seanan's thoughts as he clutched his stomach. He had not intended to dishonor himself by lying to his brother, but that is what was happening. Coming to Earth had not been simple, or fast, and there was every reason to worry.

The hard alien ground pressed into his back. Strange buildings rose around him to block out the sky and still rain managed to find his face. Confused, he tried to push up, but he was too weak from the wounds in his stomach. The magical human weapon had sounded twice with loud *pops* to create the burning holes in his body before the attackers fled. Blood ran between his fingers. How did this happen? Why had he left the portal and his companions? Why...?

And then he remembered why. His eyes moved over the wet stone path to the woman lying on the ground. A young man tenderly brushed the hair off her beaten face.

Seanan squinted, trying to see the woman through the light rainfall. Her screams had drawn him like an enchantress in need. She required help. Honor instinctively made him want to help her. No, it was more than that. Without thought, he had raced toward the noise to save her and, in doing so, he had left his people behind and broke his promise to his brother.

Galen would not know what happened. He wouldn't understand. He would be alone. Seanan needed to go home.

Human men spoke, but he comprehended very little of the Earth language dialect. Between the knowledge of the elders and the limited information shared by the Reticulans, he had thought he would understand more. He glanced around in confusion. Three men had come to rescue the woman seconds after Seanan's arrival. They didn't appear to want him dead.

"Brian, are they gone?" the oldest male demanded as he came to stand over Seanan.

"Yes, Dad, they're gone," Brian said from the far end of the alley, his voice gruff.

"Rory, is she alive?" the one called Dad yelled to the man by the woman.

"I think so," Rory answered.

"What is he?" Brian asked. The question was joined by the sound of footsteps running toward them.

"I Seanan of," Seanan tried to speak. He began frantically trying to tell them he needed to get to the portal before it closed, but the sound of the Draig language only caused strange expressions to form on their features.

"Sean?" the older man repeated, cautiously kneeling beside him. "Your name is Sean?"

"Seanan." Seanan nodded as he struggled to stand. He had to get to the portal. He needed to go home.

"He saved me." Brian, who had been the target of the magic hole maker, appeared. "We have to help him."

"Easy, Sean." Dad held him down but didn't look as if he tried to hurt him as he examined the stomach wounds. "You took the bullets meant for my son. I don't know what you are, but the Flahertys owe you. I promise we will keep you safe."

"What do we do?" Brian asked. "The hospitals will have questions and—"

Seanan again tried to stand. They kept speaking, but he couldn't understand what all of the strange sounds meant. He didn't want to be here. His eyes flashed to the woman, wondering how he could carry her to the portal and still make it home before it closed. He saved her, and it was his duty to protect her. Plus, something about her voice stirred his emotions. He didn't have time to analyze the connection.

"Keep still," the older man ordered.

Seanan was torn about what to do next, even as he lay dying on the ground. He wanted to go home to his brother to keep his promise. He wanted to go to the woman. He needed to get her help. He needed to get her. He needed her. He needed...her. Loss of blood made him lightheaded, and it became hard to concentrate.

"Look at him try to leave. He clearly doesn't want a hospital." The older man pressed his hands to Seanan's stomach and firmly held him down. "Brian, go get the car. We'll take him to Jake. He won't ask questions. This man saved your life. We owe him."

"What about the woman?" Brian asked as he sprinted down the alley.

"Rory?" the man at his stomach yelled. "You got her?"

"That monster saved her." Rory supported the woman's head with his hands.

"Don't call him that. We don't know what he is," Dad ordered.

"Well, that's one hell of a birth defect," Rory answered.

"He looks human now," Dad observed. "Will she live?"

"She's breathing, but she needs a doctor," Rory said.

"Call it in and get her to the hospital. Stay with her until we get there." The man trained his eyes on Seanan as if forcing him to meet his gaze. "We'll figure the rest out later."

"Her," Seanan mumbled in the broken Earth language. "Need. Her."

"Try not to move," Dad ordered. "You're going to be all right."

GILROY, *Massachusetts, Earth, Two Years Later...*

"Get out of the car."

Sean Flaherty stiffened at the soft whisper, but pretended not to hear it. Irritation quickly replaced the initial moment of shock. After spending the last two nights searching all the bars in the district of Olde Village for a missing bail bond that hadn't shown up for court, he simply wasn't in the mood. The bondsman who hired him would be out a barrel of Earth dollars if Sean didn't find accused drug dealer, Dougie Sinclair, within the next four days. He sure as hell wasn't going to lose Duncan's car on top of everything else.

Sean owed the Flaherty family his life. Upon arriving through the portal, he'd heard a woman in trouble and had run to help, but shifting into dragon form had prompted her assailants to turn their anger on him instead. His appearance had saved her life, and he took two bullets meant for the off duty and slightly drunk police officer, Brian Flaherty. At the time, he hadn't realized he was taking bullets, or what bullets even were. Regardless, that act secured him a safe place and friends on a new planet. If not for the family patriarch, Duncan Flaherty, insisting they take him to a private doctor and thus keeping him out of the public system, he never would have survived.

Modern human culture turned out to be nothing like the Draig had predicted. Humans didn't even know that shifters or dragons were real. The castles had transformed into clusters of towers and buildings. Humans had evolved into a society ruled by science and something called the Internet. Sean hated the Internet.

Luckily, his natural abilities as a shifter gave him unique skills. The dragon-shift could help him to defend himself from a fatal attack—not that he should shift in front of humans—and a heightened sense of smell and sight helped him track fugitives. In such ways, he was superior to humans, a hunter tracking prey.

Unless he was tired, apparently. How else was this criminal getting the jump on him?

Sean stuck the key into the ignition and pretended he didn't hear the words. He watched through his rear-view mirror as a dark figure in baggy clothes crouched along the convertible's side. The fast hunched walk and directness in which the person moved made their intent unmistakable. Sean didn't turn around as he slowly grabbed the door handle and waited. Talons extended from his fingertips, the dragon inside him eager to strike. He scanned the area in the rear-view mirror, determining the guy worked alone.

The would-be robber came up too fast for Sean to get out of the car so he waited. Hard metal pressed against the back of his skull. Unfortunately for the thief, he was trying to carjack the wrong man's vehicle at the wrong time. It was three o'clock in the morning. Completely exhausted and in need of a bed, Sean wasn't about to let some jerk-off steal his ride home.

Sean forced down the natural impulse to shift fully. He needed to keep the dragon hidden. Earth people thought he was a myth, and it was better if he kept it that way. He retracted his talons and instead reached for the handgun concealed between the driver's seat and the center console.

"I said, get out of the car!" The brusque voice grew louder than before, and the gun barrel slipped against his head.

Sean didn't hesitate. He whipped around to face his attacker, bumping open the door with his thigh while swiping at the gun hand. A surprised feminine cry preceded the light sound of something hitting the leather of his seat. The fact the criminal turned out to be a woman didn't stop him. It had been a hard lesson that Earth women were not the delicate creatures his people believed them to be. The dragon-shifter females of the past generations were strong, but humans were supposed to be fragile because of their inability to shift. However, there was nothing fragile about many of the Bostonian women he'd met.

Pointing his gun at her, he growled, "And I say get on the ground. Now."

She didn't obey. He glanced into the car for her weapon, but instead found a tube of lipstick on the front seat. The unmistakable metal case gleamed. She'd tried to rob him with female face paint?

Decorative wrought iron streetlights illuminated the brick-lined road to cast shadows over her features. The woman's blue eyes stared at him from beneath the shade of the black sweatshirt's hood. Her gaze went first to his gun and then back to his face. A wisp of blonde bangs fell long against her pale cheek.

"Jules?" The air left his lungs, and he couldn't breathe. It had been two years, and she'd been more of a brunette, but he knew her face. In fact, he'd never forgotten it. How could he? She was the reason he couldn't go home.

At the sound of his voice, she blinked in surprise, her eyes darting up to his. Vulnerability passed over her features, quickly hidden behind a hard mask. When she spoke, the low flat tone gave nothing away, "Sean."

Sean aimed his gun to the side, unable to keep the weapon drawn. The distant formality in her voice surprised him, almost as much as the hold-up. "What are you doing here? What happened to you? You came to see me when I was recovering, and I thought there was something between us but you never returned. Two years later you come to rob me of my car?"

"If it makes you feel better, I didn't know it was you or your car." Her voice sounded the same though her Massachusetts accent seemed lighter. Jules glanced back in agitation. There was no happy reunion in her tone, no surprise or remorse. "You sound different than I remember." She glanced over his clothes. "You look different too."

When he'd arrived, Sean had spoken an antiquated version of Earth English. The loose fitted pants and tunic shirt of his people made him look like some kind of cult member. Even his gestures and mannerisms set him apart as strange. "I was new to Southie."

Southie was what those in the densely populated area of South Boston called home, a blue-collar, Irish-Catholic neighborhood located south of Fort Point Channel and flanking Dorchester Bay. It was also where the portal from his home world had dropped him off, and where Sean now lived hidden amongst the locals. He made it his business to walk every inch of his new neighborhood to learn his surroundings. Every stone, every blade of grass, every neon light was emblazoned into his mind. He even visited where the portal had appeared, hoping his people would come back. They had not.

Southie streets and alleys had welcomed him in the darkness as he tried to forget the life he'd left behind. He found himself restless, partly empty, always looking around, not knowing what he searched for. It wasn't hard to disappear in Boston.

The city's population allowed him to fade into the crowds.

"You look like a Flaherty," she said.

"That is what I am called. Sean Flaherty." The light Boston Irish burr of his Earth family had thickened Sean's accent, softening his "r" to an "h", since they had been the ones to teach him how to blend in with the locals.

"Put the gun down, Sean Flaherty. You won't shoot me." Jules was right. He wouldn't hurt her. Every fiber of his being screamed to protect her.

"What's going on? If you're in trouble, I can help you." Sean had imagined seeing her again, but never like this. She had changed little in appearance, aside from the hard expression. She was still thin, still aggressive in stance and still one of the most beautiful women he'd ever seen. He couldn't help but wonder what the years had done to turn her from a sweet, nervous woman coming to thank him for saving her life into this hard-faced criminal trying to jack him of his car.

"Still trying to save the world? You're a little out of your superhero jurisdiction." She gave a small laugh and pointed north. "Boston's twenty minutes that way."

"I'm not a superhero." He studied her attractive

face, unable to believe he was finally seeing her again. He'd hoped this moment would happen. "I have seen the action movies you speak of, but Brian says those men are not real."

"Your humor is a little odd, isn't it? That's not an insult. I don't mind. Craziest thing, that night when you came to help me I would have sworn you were a comic book hero." She studied his face. "But it was dark and raining, and I had suffered a blow to my head."

"I don't understand. You are not crazy."

"I thought you were some kind of dinosaur man or dragon man. I saw you coming from the darkness to defend my honor. When Brian showed, you stepped in front of a gun to save him." She made a small noise. "I don't know why we're talking about this. I don't have time."

"Jules, tell me what is happening—"

Jules struck with lightning speed, spinning to knee him in the gut. Sean buckled in surprise, dropping his gun. He suppressed the urge to shift, knowing he could subdue her within seconds if he wanted. She drew her elbow down hard on his shoulder. He fell to his knees, pain shooting through his stomach and neck. She shoved past him into the driver's seat and had the car into reverse before he could even stand.

"By the way, I still appreciate what you did for me in that alley. Sorry about the car." Tires screeched as she took off.

Disbelief filled him. Sean pushed up from the brick street only to sit on the curb. Jules was back in his life, and she'd hit him? Emotions overwhelmed him as they had the night he'd come to Earth. Her voice stirred something primal deep inside his soul. Thoughts of her clouded his mind, and he stared after the taillights to watch the only woman he would ever love steal his car.

"I do not know what the gods were thinking when they brought me to you, Jules Dalton."

3

JULES DALTON GASPED for breath as Sean's figure disappeared from the rear-view mirror. Her memory of him had not done him justice. Muscles rippled over his arms and beneath his white t-shirt. His shoulders were broader than she remembered and his hair shorter. Brown waves framed his eyes, reaching his temples. They had only known each other briefly, but it had been enough to burn him into her memory. He'd saved her life and had almost lost his because of it.

There was no time to explain what was happening, and she definitely didn't want him getting involved. She owed a great deal to the Flahertys, a family of Irish cops from Boston, but mostly she owed Sean. Duncan, the Flaherty patriarch, had told her Sean was some kind of relative—maybe a nephew?—when he'd come to her in the hospital to take her statement. She'd been a little out of it at the time, so painkillers and shock hazed the details of the conversation. Although, she did remember trying to convince Duncan and Brian that she'd seen a dinosaur-man.

What she did know is that Sean exuded a certain protectiveness, one she had almost mistaken for love when she'd gone to thank him. He'd been on a bed in the Flaherty home, bandaged around his stomach, and still he insisted on trying to stand when she entered the room. Bed sheets twisted around his hips. Concerned eyes met hers. He was her superhero. She owed him everything. The rush of feelings she'd had for him had poured over her like the ocean, the waves crashing on her head. Luckily, Duncan had set her straight before she made a complete ass of herself. Apparently, it was common for victims of crimes to form attachments to their rescuers. It happened to cops all the time.

Still, Sean had been a hard one to get over. Even now the rush came back, and she found herself gasping for breath. He saved her life, and she owed it to him to make it a meaningful life.

As if stealing a car wasn't enough of a rush, now

she had to contend with memories best left buried. The combination made her emotions a jumbled mess. After all this time, he still made her heart beat faster just by looking at her with those piercing green eyes. If someone had asked her last week if she was over him, she'd have said, "yes," without question. But seeing him tonight, his muscular physique and devilishly handsome face, she knew in reality that wasn't the case. There had to be a reason why she hadn't looked at another man since him. Her subconscious mind still believed she was in love with Sean.

Stealing a souped-up muscle car wasn't the smartest move for someone who wanted to lie low, but what it lacked in subtlety it more than made up for in speed—should the need arise. Plus, she hadn't expected the car's owner to be Sean, but rather a sniveling rich boy who'd cry and lay on the ground as she made a getaway. She could only hope that Sean wouldn't report her to his family, but would instead come after the car himself. By then, she'd be long gone, but not involving the authorities would make her escape all the easier. With what she was running from, the police couldn't protect her, not even the entire Flaherty clan of cops. There was also no guarantee that the police would *want* to protect her. The line between good and bad often became blurred, and she didn't know whom to trust.

"Stop over-thinking, Jules. No one saw you."

Though, in a way, she almost preferred a police chase to seeing Sean again. Jules took another deep breath, and continued to mumble to herself.

"They don't know you were there. They don't know you have evidence. You're safe. The video is safe."

She glanced at the rearview mirror but Sean was no longer in sight.

"Sean's fine. He can take care of himself."

She shifted gears, easing down the street.

"You just need to play it safe and be one-hundred-and-fifty-thousand percent sure before you make a move."

The conversation with herself wasn't helping ease the fear knotted in her stomach.

Vehicles sped by her, but she kept her speed only a mile over the limit. The windshield prevented the breeze from hitting her directly, but with the top down she was able to take in the much-needed fresh air. Music blared from inside a passing truck, the hard rock melody pumping steadily over the hum of her stolen car's engine.

Suddenly, a ring sounded from inside her sweatshirt. Jules jolted in alarm before realizing it was her phone. She pulled it from the front pocket and flipped it open to look at the caller ID.

"Unknown."

Her hand shook. She pushed the talk button and lifted the phone to her ear. She didn't speak, only listened to the dead air. Jules slowed the car for a red light. Finally, a voice purred, "Jules Dalton. You missed your shift, *princesa*."

The smooth Spanish accent of the woman's voice practically oozed from the phone. Juanita Velázquez was the oldest sibling of five. Jules speculated Juanita's callousness came from a lifetime of trying to show up her bad boy brothers. Born in America, her parents had emigrated from Spain and were, for lack of a better word, crime bosses in Boston's East Side until their death. In the years since, three of Juanita's brothers had been killed—two to gunshots and one in a mysterious fire. Rumor had it that Juanita was behind the murders. Anyone who looked into Juanita's eyes would believe her capable. It was as if a piece of her soul had been carved out and thrown away. Her remaining sibling, baby brother Hector, obeyed her like an abused child trying to please his mommy.

"Family emergency." Jules glanced nervously around to see if she was being followed.

"Did you think you could run? Did you think we wouldn't find out what you've been up to?"

"Sorry, *chica*, you must have the wrong number." Jules forced a lightness she didn't feel. After three days with no sleep, all she wanted to do was drive to some motel in the middle of Nowhere, USA and disappear into a bed. But, to run away forever would mean they won. She wouldn't let that happen. She would not be a victim. Never again.

Juanita laughed, and it was easy for Jules to picture the woman's perfectly manicured fingers tapping her flawless chin beneath full red lips. Dark and exotic, Juanita looked more like a model than a criminal. In some ways, Jules knew that is what made her so deadly. The woman would smile prettily, even as she whipped a gun from behind her back and shot down whoever was in her way.

"Where are you going?" Juanita asked. A horn honked behind Jules, alerting her to the changed light. "Come back to Boston. Let's have a conversation. I'm sure we can come to an arrangement. All we want is the recording."

Jules answered by shutting her phone and tossing it on the seat next to the silver lipstick container.

Juanita's "arrangement" would be Jules's dead body at the bottom of the Charles River.

She stepped on the gas, zooming down the street toward the edge of town. If she didn't sleep soon, she'd likely crash. Already she felt her senses dulling. The fact that she could be so tired despite Juanita's phone call spoke volumes.

She'd have to figure out somewhere to ditch the phone, but not until she picked up a burner phone, and perhaps a gun. The lipstick tube hold-ups weren't going to get her too far. If Sean had put up a fight, her escape would have already been over. But she understood what type of man he was well enough to know if she hit him, he wouldn't strike back.

With limited money at her disposal, she had to plan wisely. Thinking of cash, she glanced around the car. Maybe Sean had a stash somewhere.

"Forgive me, dinosaur-man, but I'm going to have to steal from you again."

4

"No, DON'T REPORT IT STOLEN." Sean glanced around the parking lot as he cut across to a side street. Drunks milled along the brick-lined strip, filling the air with bouts of robust laughter. A fight broke out further down the block. Sean ignored it, turning his back on the brawl. It reminded him of his home world when camping and drinking inevitably turned into sport.

He knew he could trust the oldest Flaherty brother to help. Since Sean had saved Brian's life, Brian treated him like a member of his family. "Just make a few calls and see if you can find out where she's going. You can track the personal GPS you gave me for your tree worship ceremony last year. It's in my bag in the trunk."

"It's called Christmas," Brian corrected.

"Yes, and I think it is honorable to celebrate the sacrifice nature has made to sustain human culture."

"I can never tell if you are messing with me, or if we did an appalling job of explaining things." Brian gave a small laugh.

"What you didn't explain I learned from the DVDs Rory gave me," Sean answered.

"Oh, man, now I know we did a horrible job explaining things," Brian mumbled. "Ok, listen, Earth women don't like to be treated like that, and a secretary's clothes doesn't fall off when she walks into her boss's office."

"Untrue," Sean countered. "Suzette's clothes often fall off when she is alone with Gus in his office. I can hear them before I walk into the building to retrieve my assignments."

"Unit Bail Bonds Gus?" Brian laughed. "Ugh, great. Some images can never be unseen. Also, your hearing is scary. You better not be listening inside my house."

"I'm on Elm Street. Where now?" Sean interrupted the banter.

"Go five blocks North. You'll come across a diner that's open all night. Wait there and I'll get you the information you need as soon as I can. I'm tracking your car now." Brian cleared his throat. "Ok, seriously, you have to tell me what happened. How did sweet little Jules steal your car? What did she say? What did you say? You didn't go all dragon and scare her, did you?"

"I do not understand what happened. One second she was there, the next she was gone." Sean rubbed his stomach and tried to ignore his aching neck. *Sweet* wasn't a word he'd use for her at the moment. "Just find her."

"Wait until I tell Dad about this tomorrow," Brian continued.

"I can imagine what your account of the story will be," Sean grumbled. By the time it made the rounds through the close-knit family, the version will have gone from Jules stealing his car to Jules left him hogtied naked in front of Faneuil Hall with spanking marks across his ass before taking off in his car. "Just call me when you find her. I'll deal with Jules."

"Jules a car thief. I still can't believe it. Want me to run her name to check if I can find out more about what's going on with her?"

Sean considered saying no, but instead found himself answering, "Yes, but only because I wish to make sure she is safe. Not because I wish to disrespect her privacy." He took a deep breath. "I want to end this call now."

"Be safe, Sean. I'll call back soon." Brian said before hanging up the phone.

Even in his irritation, worry filled him. There were so many unanswered questions, but even more answers he wished didn't exist. His understanding of women in general was limited, not to mention that of Earth women. It's not like he'd had females in abundance on his home world to practice interacting with. When she'd visited him after her attack, Duncan had said Sean confused her gratitude for something more and that he should leave her be. Saving a woman did not give him the right to her.

With two gunshot wounds, he'd been in no condition to chase after Jules. When finally he could make his way around Boston alone, he'd looked for her. All he found was an empty apartment.

Time had helped him to understand human ways, but he still couldn't figure out what he'd done or said to make Jules disappear without coming back to see him. Despite Duncan's advice on women, Sean was sure he had a connection with Jules. He felt it again tonight. The invisible thread pulled from inside her body to lasso him in. Had she asked, he would have made her his mate without thought—even though she didn't know he was a dragon-shifter, and she was a car thief. None of that mattered to his heart.

Sean closed his eyes.

"*Perdón*, did that chick say where she was going with your car?" The light Spanish accent rolled effortlessly from beside him.

"I didn't ask." Sean frowned, turning to look at the sedan progressing slowly beside him on the street. It had been trailing him for a couple of blocks, but he wasn't in the mood for conversation.

A man smiled and opened the car door. The vehicle stopped to allow him to step out. His face was somewhat familiar though Sean was sure he'd never met him before. He wore a casual white linen shirt with embroidery up one side, open over a white t-shirt and a dark pair of denim jeans. Thick dark brown hair was slicked back, cropped short around the nape and kept longer on top. The car pulled next to the curb, and two men joined them, holding back like bodyguards. Their thick arms crossed over their chests, and they had apparently mastered the art of the dead stare.

"Why? You know her?" Sean asked.

"You could say that."

"Who are you?" Sean crossed his arms, mimicking the aggressive posture. A few humans didn't frighten him. One shift and he'd tear them apart.

"I am Hector. Don't worry, *hombre*, we'll find your car." Hector motioned to his thugs. One reached into his jacket and pulled out a business card. He handed the card forward to Hector, who took it between two fingers and then offered it to Sean with a sweeping flick of his wrist. "Here is my number. You call me if you see her again or if that friend of yours on the phone tracks her down. She is very dangerous. Don't underestimate her." Hector glanced over Sean. "But you look like you can handle yourself. There's a reward if you detain her for me."

Sean pocketed the card without reading it. He didn't like knowing this Hector had been eavesdropping on his conversation. "Are you a bounty hunter?"

Hector gave a small laugh. "Something like that. Do what's right. If you see her again, call me. A dangerous woman like that shouldn't be out roaming the streets." The man straightened his shoulders, adjusting his shirt with a long-armed gesture before turning in a dramatic display clearly intended to make his presence known to the world. To his men, he said, "*Vámonos*. Come on." The goons trailed behind him like obedient dogs as they all got back in the car.

Sean frowned, keeping an eye on them as they drove away. Maybe he didn't understand Jules as well as he thought.

5

"FUCKING SHIT!" Jules paced the small motel room off the highway, staring at the open leather messenger bag on the bed. It would seem Sean had switched professions from superhero to bounty hunter as signified by the giant stack of bail bond files in his trunk. It seemed odd to be a bounty hunter in the Flaherty family of police. Though, Sean had never said he was a cop. She'd just assumed.

She'd flipped through his files and saw the type of bonds his employers wrote—drug dealers, gang bangers, and general lowlifes. Many of them had overdue court dates and were out running free. She couldn't believe it. Not only had he quit being a superhero, but it also seemed he now helped the bastards back out onto the streets. How could he be part of the system that freed criminals after one had shot him?

"Maybe I was wrong about him," she mused, a sense of disappointment and remorse washing over her. Though, she shouldn't be too surprised. She'd often wondered how Brian, Rory, and Duncan had happened to be by the exact alleyway where she was attacked on their day off. Of course, she had no proof of corruption and wrongdoing, but sometimes it felt as if there were a thin line between cops and criminals.

It hurt to think of the past. Where once her heart held so much promise and hope, there was now only a coldness she couldn't shake. A part of her had died —a vital, loving, optimistic part. One night changed it all. She used to wish she could take her thumb and blot out that whole day from her personal timeline.

"Quit dwelling," she ordered herself, squashing her emotions until only the calmness remained. "It is better this way. I'm in control. I will not be a victim. I will not sleepwalk through life. I depend only on myself."

Jules put everything back into the leather bag except the roll of money she'd found. The cash, she stuffed into her hooded sweatshirt's pocket. It was enough to keep her going for weeks, so long as she kept a low profile. She promised herself she'd pay Sean back if she lived.

Slipping the sweatshirt off her head, she was careful to keep the cash safely inside the pocket as she laid it on the table next to the new phone and the bag of groceries she'd purchased from a convenience store. Since she'd been leaving the gym when Juanita's thugs had tried to invite her into their car, she hadn't had time to change out of her sweaty workout gear. Paranoid, Jules was convinced they had been trailing her through Boston for the past three days, until she managed to hitch a ride to Gilroy. Juanita's call confirmed they were after her.

The tight black tank top with built-in bra reeked of stale sweat. Jules pulled the tank over her head, glad to be rid of it. She stretched her arms and crossed the room half-naked. The exercise pants were little better, and she slid them off her hips, taking the cotton panties and socks with them.

Jules ignored her reflection in the mirror, no longer one of those women who spent hours dwelling over her appearance. Keeping her body toned wasn't out of vanity, but necessity. With nothing else to put on, she took dish soap out of the grocery bag and headed toward the shower to do her laundry while she bathed. The soap was the closest thing she could find to detergent, and the smell of lemon-lime was definitely better than body odor.

Hot water felt great, even if the only soap available was the cheaply scented motel brand that claimed to be lavender infused. The combination shampoo/conditioner was harsh, and she'd be fighting to brush her hair of the tangles it made. Still, beggars couldn't be choosers.

Jules ran her hands down her stomach, only to stiffen as Sean came to mind. He was broader than she remembered, forged with muscles, or had she erased that detail of him over the years? A maturity radiated from his face, both formidable and confident. When she'd met him at the Flaherty house, she remembered thinking he stared at everything in wonder, as if seeing it for the first time, almost like a child stepping out into the world. Or maybe that was the painkillers he'd undoubtedly been on.

Her sex tingled, despite the fatigue in her limbs. Already she knew his body would feel perfect against hers. The sensation curled its way up to her breasts, branching toward her erect nipples. Did she indulge the fantasy by allowing herself to think about him? Was it a mistake to feel this much? Even as she made the decision to stop, her hand brushed lower between her thighs.

Just a couple strokes, she told herself.

Her finger slid along her folds, rubbing the tender bud. She gasped lightly, pinching a nipple as the hot water hit her chest. Her fingers were a sorry replacement for a man and the harder she tried to find release, the more her sex ached to be filled with thick, hard flesh. She jerked, the movements between her hips and hand becoming like a battle neither could win.

"Damn, I need to be held," she whispered as if the soft admission would somehow make the desire a fact. Jules tried to imagine a faceless stranger next to her body, but Sean's face came to mind. Still, the idea of him wasn't enough. She tried to climax, fought for it, but in the end, the tiny, unsatisfactory tremors caused more disappointment than release.

After washing her clothes and hanging them over the shower rod to air dry, she toweled off, jerked the tangles from her hair with violent strokes and went to bed naked. She'd give herself one night of rest before getting back on the road.

6

SEAN TIPPED the motel desk clerk before taking the room key from him. Brian had tracked the car, and it hadn't taken Sean long to discover it hidden behind the motel under the limb-cast shadows of the parking lot. Once he found the car, he'd dismissed the taxi that had been driving him around for the last several hours. The clerk claimed he hadn't seen Jules at the hotel before she checked in that night. That was something. At least she wasn't living in the rundown facility.

Sean's initial surprise had turned to irritation, then anger, until finally settling into an exhausted frustration.

Streaks of dawn filtered over the sky in brilliant magenta and orange, as he gripped the metal key.

Lifting his hand to knock on the door, he paused. What if she wasn't alone in the room? Leaning his ear to the cold, hard surface, he listened. The soft sound of voices spoke over a musical background signifying the television was on. He took a deep breath, trying to detect her scent. The dumpster down the block was too overpowering.

"She stole my car, after all," he justified to himself, slipping the key quietly into the lock. Sean glanced up and down the empty walkway in front of the rooms. He turned the knob, pushing in.

Blue light from the television illuminated the gloomy motel room. With a worn dresser, bed, and nightstand, it seemed a bleak place. Dwellings like this made him miss the fresh air and open fields of home. Sure, Earth had areas of open nature, but it was a different environment. He found it difficult to become accustomed to the small things. Tree bark had a less bubbled, jagged texture. Darkness fell every night, not just once a year, and the planet only had one yellow sun, not two yellows and a blue. It meant daylight was no longer tinted with green, but a brighter white. And a night of darkness was no longer a special occasion to go camping with his brother for it happened every sunset.

His breath caught as his gaze stopped on the bed.

Suddenly, the location didn't appear to be so depressing.

The television light flashed, changing colors as it caressed Jules's naked flesh. The long, sleek lines of her muscles caused his fingers to flex and his desire for her to stir. Red danced along the smooth slope of her tanned, firm ass. It faded to green as his eyes slid up her back over the crevice of her spine and the roundness of her shoulder. Blue flashed again, drawing Sean from his stupor. He quickly shut the door behind him. Here, like this, she looked so fragile.

In some ways, as he walked toward the bed, it was as if no time had passed. He felt like he had the first evening of his arrival when he heard her voice calling out. One sound and he became connected. She was his siren, his enchantress. He could take on any Earthling in a fight and win, but Jules would defeat him every time with a single glance.

His dragon senses had detected her desire for him in the past, even if she never acted on it. What would it be like between them? Every instinct tingled as if to say he had a right to look at her, to touch her, to claim her.

But this was not his home world. Humans did not abide by dragon-shifter rules. He should turn away and bury the instincts screaming inside his body.

Sean forgot about his car. He pressed his knee into the bed, hovering his hand over her damp hair. She gave a soft moan, adjusting her hips without waking to look at him.

No part of touching her felt wrong. A trance came over him. The primal part of his dragon whispered in his ear. Where he'd experienced loneliness and homesickness moments before, he now felt hope. She was fire in the darkness, drawing him toward her light.

His hand hovered along her back before making contact with her side. The smooth curve of her ass and hip drew his caress before he skimmed over the back of her thigh. She moaned, a welcoming sound. He should have acted on instinct years before when she came to thank him. He dipped his fingers between her legs, traveling upward toward her cleft. A light tremor worked along her body, but she didn't pull away.

Her silky flesh glided beneath the pads of his fingertips. When he pushed between her thighs, the heat of her sex warmed the side of his hand even as the soft curls tickled his skin. Jules squirmed, wiggling ever so slightly on the bed. He detected the faintest traces of lavender and lemon but beyond that the smell of woman. Leaning his face next to her back, he took in her scent. This was the reaction he longed for.

Sean released a slow breath against her, blowing warmth and watching as goose bumps formed. This time, when Jules moved, it was to turn over with a jerk. Her hand struck out, aimed for his throat. She clutched a sharp steak knife. Sean grabbed her wrist, tugging it to the side and shaking it once, so the blade fell from her fingers. Jules's chest thrust into his. Sean nudged the knife, sending it over the side of the bed with a light clank.

"That's twice you've threatened my life," he said. "At least you used a real weapon and not face paint."

Her aggressiveness teased the hunter in him. Blue eyes narrowed, and if he wasn't mistaken, she growled in the back of her throat in anger. "What are you doing here, superhero?"

"Taking what's mine." Sean had meant his car, but as he said the words he couldn't help glancing to her mouth. He wanted to kiss her, to feel her. Grabbing her by the side of her face, he held her by her hair. Until that moment, he didn't realize how much he'd yearned for her.

She tried to pull her hand away to fight. "You can't just break into my room."

"Just like you can't steal my car?" He lowered his tone. "Should we call the police, Jules? Let them figure it out?"

"Go ahead. I'll deny taking your car. This is my room. You're the one breaking and entering." She seemed unaware that she was vulnerable and naked. He was barely aware of anything else.

"I'll just say you were harboring a fugitive," he countered. His mouth opened wide, and he angled his head as if to consume her. Instead, he denied himself the kiss. "I see you went through my bag."

Jules gave a weak laugh, her body relaxing some. "The superhero I remembered wouldn't be helping bad guys out of jail."

"The Jules I know wouldn't have stolen my car." He didn't intend for his words to sound mean, but her expression hardened. Her icy stare had started to thaw, but now all signs of softness disappeared.

"I guess that just means we don't know each other at all. It doesn't matter. This isn't a reunion. I don't want to talk about the past. The Jules you met was messed up in the head. You don't know me, and I don't know you." She pushed hard, freeing her wrist.

Sean refrained from pointing out that she'd

started the conversation about the past. Besides, how could they not talk about it? It was how they had met.

Jules tried to stand, but Sean stopped her. "Then tell me about the new Jules. What's going on? Why did you steal my car?"

"I," she leaned her face into his, her tone sultry, "needed..."

Sean's breath caught and his lids fell heavy over his eyes. By all the universes, this woman had a hold on him since the very first second he'd heard her scared voice echoing in the night. Did she know the power she held?

"A car," she finished in a whisper. Television light moved over her naked body like see-through silk, swimming over her flesh, urging his hands to do the same.

Sean closed the distance, unable to resist any longer. His lips met hers, instantly parting. Hunger and need raged through him, causing his ordinarily graceful movements to be jerking and desperate. Her lips tasted like mint and promise—the kind of promise he hadn't felt since stepping through the portal. The warm glide of her tongue danced along his, twirling and thrusting.

He cupped her breast, running his palm over the soft mound. Her nipple hardened. A soft groan sounded, but he wasn't sure if it came from his throat or hers.

Jules tugged at his waist, thankfully as eager as he. Sean lifted from the bed, standing on his knees. She tugged his pants down, freeing his arousal. Warm fingers glided up the top curve of his ass as she too stood on her knees, facing him. She shoved her hands down, squeezing his cheeks and forcing his hips forward. The softness of her stomach rubbed along his length, and he almost came from that first contact.

"Ah!" His head tilted back on his shoulders as he gasped. He rocked his hips against her at a feverish pace. A ripple worked over his body, causing his fingertips to begin to shift. He forced the dragon back inside, hiding it.

"Ah, shit," she swore. There was nothing sweet and slow about the way she fell back on the bed, angling her legs apart. Jules grabbed his shirt, pulling him forward between her thighs. She reached for his shaft, angling it toward her sex. "Fuck me."

His jeans still clinging to his upper thighs, he lifted himself up and delved forward. This was not how he imagined his first coupling with her, but he couldn't resist. Tight heat enveloped his length as she took him in. It felt so right that he cried out. He closed his eyes, hiding the primal shift of his dragon that would flash in his gaze.

Sean pumped his hips hard and fast, desperate to feel their connection. Blonde hair flowed in silky locks around her shoulders to her breasts. The mounds bounced with each pass of her hips and he stared greedily at them. Sean drove into her to watch them bob erotically. She met his movements, digging her fingernails into his shoulders. The material of his shirt kept them from stabbing too deep.

"Jules," he whispered. He couldn't believe this was happening.

"Ah." Her mouth opened, but no coherent words came out.

Jules gripped him tight, the muscles of her sex bearing down as she found release. The pressure became too much. His hips jerked. Suddenly, Jules pushed at his chest, forcing his body out of hers as he came. His seed spilled on the bed as she wiggled out from underneath him. He required a moment of heavy breathing before Sean came to his complete senses. He'd almost found release inside her, without thought of the consequences. But when he was inside her he felt like she was his and this is where he belonged. Evidently, by the look on her face, she wasn't feeling the same level of devotion he was. He would never understand humans. As a dragon-shifter, he trusted his feelings and did not question them. Just like the first time he'd met her, he knew. Jules had his heart.

"Your keys are on the dresser. Take your belongings and go." She sat on the bed, not looking at him, not bothering to get dressed.

The aftermath of pleasure clouded his mind, and he wanted nothing more than to hold her. "What will you do?"

"Steal another car," she answered.

His jeans pressed uncomfortably into his hips, and he stood, pulling them up over his ass. He didn't want to leave her. This was not how fate was supposed to happen. But this wasn't his planet. These were not his people. Humans did not see mating as his kind did. He had to assimilate. He had to respect what she wanted, even if it wasn't him.

"Jules, talk to me. After what we did—" He gestured toward the bed as her words cut him off.

"Don't worry about me. I'll be fine." She gave him a small smile, and it caused the ache in his chest to grow. "I know the difference between sex and love."

"Jules, I can help you," he insisted.

"You don't even know what's happening. How

can you help? Besides, by the looks of your bag, you have enough work to do." She ran her fingers over her hair, straightening and fluffing the locks.

"Those are older files. I've caught all but one of them." He waved his hand in dismissal. "It doesn't matter. Forget the files. You're in trouble."

"I can handle myself." Her nonchalant tone irked him. "I don't want you here, Sean. I'm sorry about your car. I'm sorry about—"

"Disappearing after you came to visit me? For not coming back when you said you'd see me later," he interjected, slightly peeved by her dismissal. "I looked for you after I healed."

"See you later is just an expression people say instead of goodbye. I couldn't visit you again. Seeing you would only remind me of what happened. I told you I don't want to talk about the past. I've forgotten it." Her expression said she spoke the truth, from the steadiness of her eyes to her stiff jaw. But he didn't believe it. He couldn't pinpoint why exactly, but every instinct told him she hadn't forgotten and that her pain and confusion ran deep.

"Someone who's forgotten doesn't need to claim so vehemently that they've forgotten." He pulled the card Hector had given him from his pocket. The white rectangle held only a phone number in the center in bold script. "Who is Hector? And why is he hunting you?"

"What...?" She stood, pulling a blanket up with her. "I—I don't know what you're talking about. I know no one by that name."

"That was not a skilled lie." He frowned.

"How do you know Hector?" Giving up the pretense, she hugged the blanket around her body, hiding her nakedness from him. The vulnerable act contradicted her earlier bravado.

"He approached me after you borrowed my car. He seemed very interested in tracking you down, even offered to pay me to deliver you."

"Is that why you've come?" She inhaled a shaky breath. "To claim a bounty, no matter which side of the law it's for?"

Sean paced the room, anger and frustration not too far from boiling over. "I'm not turning you in to the authorities, but I can't help you if you don't talk to me."

"Good, because I'm not looking for your help." Jules sighed, letting loose a heavy, long breath. "Just lock up when you go. Take your stuff and leave."

He opened his mouth to protest, but what could he say? Part of him wanted to jump into bed, pull her close and demand she let him take care of her. He didn't want to go. After staring at her for a long moment, he nodded. "Fine, but I'm leaving you my card. Promise me you'll call if you need anything."

Jules silently indicated that she understood.

"Do you need anything now? Money? Food?"

She shook her head in denial. "I just need you to leave."

Sean, my boy, you can't help them that won't help themselves, or so Duncan's wife, Teresa, had told him on numerous occasions.

"Jules," he hesitated. What more could he say? "Call if you need me."

7

J ULES HELD VERY STILL as Sean walked out of the motel room. She wasn't surprised that he'd found her. Finding people was what bounty hunters did.

It was also what Hector did. Only, if Hector found her, he wouldn't be as understanding as Sean. The Velázquez family scared the crap out of her. If they discovered her with Sean, they wouldn't hesitate to kill them both. No matter how much she wanted to beg Sean to stay with her, she couldn't put his life in danger.

"You pushed things too far, Jules," she scolded herself. "What is wrong with you? You've made a mess of things."

She crawled out of bed. The memory of Sean's hands still ran over her body, confusing her emotions

69

even more. She didn't need the complications of her feelings clouding what needed to be done.

It was like no time had gone by. One look, and he drew her to him. The bond that formed the first time they met was forged in something stronger than steel. She'd thought time would erase her feelings, feelings born out of gratitude and guilt and a case of victim-hero worship. That wasn't the case. Sending him away had been hard. All she wanted was to call him back to her and rest in his arms forever.

Already she missed him, the ache worse than when she walked away two years ago. What did she know about him besides ridiculous visions of a dragon man coming through the rain to save her? Even her memory of the night couldn't be trusted.

Crossing to the window, she pulled the curtain aside. Sean walked away from her, his confident body stepping from the bright section of the motel parking lot into the shadows where she'd parked his car. Why had she parked it next to the hotel where he would discover it? Was the lapse of judgment from exhaustion? Or did some secret part of her want him to find her?

"I'm a psychological mess, Sean," she whispered. "Stop trying to save me."

Jules dropped the curtain and moved to gather

her belongings. She would wait until he drove off before leaving the motel room. Her clothes were still damp, but she would put them on anyway. Sean hadn't discovered she'd taken his cash, and she could buy a change of clothes later. Right now, she needed to go.

No part of her believed Sean would leave her be now that he knew she was in trouble, and she couldn't allow him to get in her way. If she died, so be it, but she couldn't cause his death. He was the most honest, selfless person she'd ever met. She needed to know people like him were out there in the world living, even if she wasn't a part of that life.

SEAN DIDN'T LOOK BACK as he strode to his car in frustration. Why could she not feel their connection? Cursed humans! How could she be so blind to what they might be together? They'd come together in an incredible explosion of chaos and insanity. Her scent lingered on his skin. His body tingled from where they'd touched. His cock ached to do it again.

She was his.

Damn it, all.

His.

Why couldn't she see it?

Taking out his phone, he dialed Brian.

"You're a pain in the ass," Brian grumbled by way of a greeting.

"And you're just an ass," Sean answered, before immediately going into why he called. "I need to trade cars."

"You're parting with the convertible? You love that car."

Sean glanced back to the motel room. "I need something that blends in more. It's important."

"Jules?" Brian's voice sobered as if he was coming more fully awake. "You found her?"

"I need you to do one of your searches on her— deeper this time. Find out what she's been doing. I need to know what kind of trouble she's been in."

"What? After all this time, after I repeatedly offered to track her down, you're going to *finally* let me look her up? I thought you said you didn't want to invade her privacy, and that using your connections to track a woman who did not wish to be with you was too much like stalking, and she deserved to have her wishes honored to be left alone. I thought you had to trust in your gods to guide you at the right time."

Sean closed his eyes, the old lecture he'd given

Brian ringing through his head. The man had offered several times to run Jules's records for him, to track her down with Earth methods. No matter how much he wanted to say yes, he never had. She ran for a reason, and he'd been new to the planet. What did he have to offer her? He had no means, no family, and no home. His honor was tarnished by his broken promise to Galen, something he'd never be able to fix. "She's in trouble, Brian. I should have come after her sooner. Maybe my gods don't watch this planet."

"Whatever has happened to her isn't your fault. You shouldn't blame yourself. You stopped—"

"Grab a pen," Sean interrupted. "I know where we can make the trade, and I will need some cash." He thought about the lump rolled into her sweatshirt. He'd seen it when he glanced over the room. She'd stolen from him, but he didn't care. Clearly, she was desperate. If she asked, he'd give her everything he had. "I gave Jules what I had on me."

8

"Yes, ma'am, I speak the truth! They had the best pumpkin pie I've tasted this side of the Mason-Dixon." The trucker grinned, nodding his head emphatically. Raymond, or as he preferred to be called "Truckerman," Johansson had picked her up in his semi-truck as she hitchhiked alongside the highway. He hauled children's toys in the back, as evident by the giant pink teddy bear painted on the side of his long trailer, and reminded her of an unrefined Santa Claus.

The man's wiry gray beard reached his chest and twitched with his frequent and boisterous laughs. Though overbearing, the sound was cheery and unthreatening. Wrinkles ran across his face, like the many roads he'd traveled in his profession. They were etched deep, hardened by age and frozen by time. Small eyes squinted behind small round sunglasses. Jules saw them staring forward every time she glanced in his direction, but for some reason felt as if he peeked at her when she wasn't looking.

"Had this patch where you could go out into the field and pick your own pumpkin," he continued, "and they'd make you a pie right from that pumpkin. Of course, you had to go back to pick the pie up. Worked out nicely because I grabbed it in on my return trip past."

"Uh-huh," Jules said, her responses on autopilot. She tried to return his smiling expression, but between his constant chattering for the last six hours and her lack of sleep, she couldn't manage more than a single nod. It had been three days, two crappy motels and five hitchhiked rides since Sean caught up with her. She traveled in no particular direction, simply zigzagged away from Boston, only to travel toward it, then away again, continuing the indecisive pattern through Massachusetts, Rhode Island, Connecticut, Pennsylvania, New Jersey, Delaware, and Maryland. The only problem was, she was nowhere closer to deciding what she should do. Did she run? Did she try to take out the Velázquez family on her own? Go in with guns blazing and a death wish? Talk to the District Attorney? Talk to the police? Anonymously hand over what evidence she had—if she could even get her hands on it? Call Sean? Could she trust Sean? Could she trust the Flahertys? Could she trust anyone?

The only answer she knew for certain is that she wouldn't call Sean. She would never get him involved in this disaster, or in her life. Too much had happened. Too much needed to remain buried right where it was. Seeing him again had been a breath of heaven and a trip to hell. Pain filled her at the thought of his face. To love a man, still, after all these years and not be able to be with him was torture. It was a mistake to be with him, but hurt to be without him. She'd thought she'd moved past him, but seeing him, touching him, had only proven how much in denial she had been.

One thing was certain. She was definitely insane. The dreams of a half-man, half-dinosaur creature coming to save her had started up again. What was even stranger, she would constantly try to make out with the monster. Her nights were a blur of kinky dragon sex and Velázquez death threats.

No matter what happened, she would not call Sean.

"You're a quiet one," Truckerman broke into her

thoughts.

"I was thinking about dragons," she mumbled, too tired to come up with a polite lie.

"Not too long ago I came from a run in Louisiana. You won't believe what folks are saying." Truckerman launched into another story with ease. "They have themselves a bona fide Cajun lizard man living in the swamps."

Jules arched a brow at that one.

"They say he's a half-man, half-dragon, the abomination of a backwater woman and an alligator. I figure he's an ex-carnie from one of those freak shows, you know with the scaly skin or tattoos, but folks are superstitious and..."

Jules let her mind drift from the man's tall tales. She had bought new clothes at a gas station along the highway. The ankle-length orange and yellow tie-dyed peasant skirt with elastic waistband and black t-shirt was a far cry from her usual street-smart style, but she didn't care. She'd shoved everything into a new yellow messenger bag. It beat the plastic grocery sacks and rolled up sweatshirt she'd been using for luggage. The more Truckerman spoke, the tighter she hugged the bag to her stomach.

"They have those hydroponic greenhouses, too." Truckerman had changed topics. "Where the roots hang in the air never touching dirt. Don't see too many of those where I'm from. My people still farm out of the ground. Not sure I want to eat food that comes from a lab and not from the earth."

"Don't blame you." Jules didn't bother to debate the man on the value of organically grown greenhouse vegetables versus chemically sprayed field ones. She didn't care either way. Those kinds of worries were for people with nothing real to be concerned about—like being hunted by Juanita and Hector Velázquez.

"Cute petting zoo set up for the kids. Had a herd of alpacas and sheep out there," Truckerman chattered on.

Jules tuned him out for several miles before his insistent throat clearing interrupted her drifting thoughts. "Sorry?"

Truckerman chuckled. "I see I was right. I have been jawin' your ear off."

"No, it's not you. I'm just tired. You have a scheduled stop anytime soon? I need coffee." She made a show of yawning.

"Sure thing, little lady. Truck stop's ahead." He hummed something akin to a country song, though she didn't know the words, before adding, "I could use a bite myself."

9

"THEY'RE PULLING into a truck stop now," Sean said into the phone. The building split into two parts with a restaurant entrance on the right and a gas station/convenience store on the left. White paint clung to the metal structure in peeling flakes. Gas pumps were set away from the building under their own canopy. "It looks like she might switch vehicles. It's possible she's heading back toward Boston again."

"Where are you?" Brian asked. The man had met up with him to bring him an abandoned old pickup from the impound lot on the same morning Sean had left Jules in her motel room. No one would miss the vehicle and, though it drove amazingly well for its condition, he didn't like it as much as the convertible.

"Somewhere near Columbia, Maryland." Sean's

long-sleeve black knit shirt, jeans and black sneakers were purposefully nondescript. He also had the gun Brian insisted he carry. The convertible had two storage compartments. Jules only rummaged through the trunk. Under the back seat in a secret compartment, he kept a suitcase full of clothes. They came in handy for situations like this one where he found himself away from his Earth home for unexpected periods of time.

"What is she doing?"

"She's thinking. Jules once told me she likes to drive to clear her head." Sean remembered everything she'd said to him. "The longer she drives, the worse the situation. Whatever is going on with her, it's bad."

"I can't believe she hitched a ride with a trucker," Brian grumbled in clear irritation.

Sean understood the over-protectiveness in the man's tone. He felt it too.

Sean had followed Jules, watching and waiting, since he picked up her trail at the first motel. The advantage of being a dragon was that once he locked in on his target, he'd be able to find her wherever she went. He'd turned his eyes for a second at a rest stop only to discover she'd jumped from a traveling salesman's car into a semi-truck.

He hoped she would lead him to answers about what was going on with her. Instead, she traveled around in a random pattern. Before the salesman, Jules had climbed in with a priest, a family from New York, and a service repairman. He knew because Brian looked up the license plates for him. The trucker Raymond Johansson had an arrest record with a few assault charges, and several drug busts.

"What is she thinking?" Brian continued. "Had I known she headed for this kind of trouble, I would've looked her up years ago. Dad sent her to victims' services to get help. I honestly thought that would do it, but obviously it wasn't enough."

"What did you find out?" Sean asked.

"I made some calls. She has a record that starts a couple of months after you arrived. There are several trespassing charges, an alleged breaking and entering, though nothing was proven. There are a few vandalism and harassment complaints and questioning for a dozen or so other crimes. She's on a few different witness lists. Two years ago, police pulled her over in a stolen car, but the owner refused to press charges, and it slipped through the cracks. I don't see pending court dates."

"How did we not hear about this?" Sean

frowned. The woman Brian described sounded nothing like the woman he'd rescued.

"Some of the charges are in surrounding towns. Suspicious activity reports are in other districts. Nothing warranted an all city alert. Aside from a speeding ticket in our district, it seems she has steered clear of Southie."

"The few times she's gone to court, no one we know saw her," Brian continued. "There are over a half million people in the city, and she simply blended in. We have a home address for her in East Boston where she works as a waitress at one of the nightclubs, *Fuego*. Though, it makes little sense that a waitress would be on the cop's radar as much as she is. I have a friend checking into the club for me to see if there is anything there."

Sean pulled along the far edge of the gravel parking lot and slipped the gearshift into neutral, letting the pickup idle. Jules hopped out of the semi-truck, slamming the door shut behind her. A small knot unraveled inside him to see she was all right. "This is my fault. When I saved her, she became my responsibility. I should have tracked her down and kept her safe."

"Who can say what is best for a person after they face tragedy? I wish I could go back and arrest the fuckers who hurt her. If I'd been on duty, my weapon might have accidentally discharged. I'm just lucky you came when you did to save my drunken ass. If not for you..."

Sean didn't answer as Brian's words trailed off. He kept his eyes steadily on Jules and turned off the engine. She and the trucker walked to the restaurant door.

"But we can't go back," Brian said. "At least they're rotting in jail."

"Not for what they did to her. For that, you should have let me kill them." Sean grabbed his wallet off the dash and stepped out of the car. He pushed it into his back pocket, opposite the gun he had strapped to his lower back. He kept a steady eye on Jules. She carried her bag with her. Would this be it? Was she meeting up with someone? Was the trucker in on it?

"She didn't want to testify," Brian inserted. "We couldn't make her give a full statement, and it took a lot of maneuvering to convince her you weren't a dragon-shifter. The doctors would have thought she was crazy and had her put under evaluation. And it's not like we could bring you forward to prove she was telling the truth. What would've been the point? Why put her through hell when the result is the same. Frankie, Joey and Sammy Boy are all doing life without parole for that spree of murders. Her reliving her pain wouldn't change that."

Taking his black leather jacket, Sean slipped it over his shoulders to hide the weapon while switching the phone between his hands. The distinct sound of the slamming truck door reverberated before being replaced by the swooshing hum of passing cars on the nearby highway. "I respect your laws even if I don't understand them. Men like that do not deserve to live. I should have killed them."

"Quit blaming yourself." Brian's audible sigh sounded through the phone. "You saved my life. You saved Jules."

"They shouldn't have needed saving in the first place."

"The police did their job when they arrested them, and the information they found on those three losers led us to other criminals. It is not our fault they were bonded out and skipped bail. Cops arrest people, Sean, and it's all they can do. Bounty hunters bring back the ones who try to get away. We are not responsible for their crimes. All we can do is what we're doing."

"It wasn't supposed to be like this," Sean answered, sorrow gripping him. His soul had been asleep since Jules walked away from him. Over the years, he'd buried what he felt, all the hurt and fear, but seeing her, touching her, smelling and tasting her, caused his pain to surge forth from its shallow grave to spill over into his chest. There was no running, no hiding, not from a pain like this. "I was supposed to be here for a few minutes. I wasn't supposed to stay. It was going to be back and forth, through the portal, simple and fast."

"I'm glad you're here."

"I do not mean to sound ungrateful for what your family has done for me. But my brother was waiting for me to return. I am sure he thinks I am dead." Sean thought of his promise to Galen. "I wish to end this call now."

"Wait, Sean," Brian interjected. "Try to focus on Jules. She needs you more than ever. Every instinct I have tells me she's lost."

Sean recognized the warning in the man's tone. "What else did you find?"

"I ran that name, 'Hector,' by some of the guys. I will not lie to you. It's not good. That card you gave me is the calling card of Hector Velázquez, the baby brother of the Velázquez crime family—the only surviving male. He's been in Spain for the last several years overseeing the family's interests there and just returned to the States. That's why none of us have seen his mug around. Word on the street is Juanita sends in Baby Hector to do cleanup. Those two goons with him are Jose G and Big Stewie. They own the club Jules was working at. If Hector is looking for her, the Velázquez family wants her dead. Or worse."

Sean felt his heart drop. "I knew Hector appeared familiar. He looks like his older brothers. I saw their pictures in the paper."

"He has twice as much to prove," Brian warned. "Be careful of him. He won't think twice about killing you if you get in his way. With his connections, he can be out of the country before the bullet even hits."

Before coming to this planet, Sean had thought dragon politics were complicated. He still didn't understand all the nuances of Earth customs, but if Brian said it was bad, it was bad.

"Why's he after her?" Sean strolled toward the glass door leading into the convenient store area of the building. He'd make his way over to the restaurant so Jules wouldn't see him.

"Don't know yet. I have some of the guys putting feelers out for more information. I'll let you know what I come up with."

"Thanks." He lowered his voice so no one in the

busy store would hear him as he pretended to look at a display of state-themed snow globes. "Call me the second you learn anything. I'm going to see if I can get her out of here without creating a scene."

"When you get her, bring her home. She's safer with a bunch of cops than out on the street. We can protect her." Brian paused. "What do you want to do about that bond of yours, Dougie? You only have a day left to get him."

"I'll call in a couple of favors for an extension. He's not violent, just an idiot middleman. His connections won't trust him with more product, so he's inconsequential. If worse comes to worse, I'll pay out the bond on him and get him later, so Gus isn't out the money."

"You don't have fifty thousand dollars to throw around," Brian reminded him. "It will wipe out your savings and most likely get your right to hunt revoked."

"So what," Sean answered. He couldn't think about that now. "This is Jules we're talking about. Fuck Dougie Sinclair. I'm not failing her."

10

NOW THAT THEY sat across from each other at the small brown table in the private truckers' section of the truck stop restaurant, Jules didn't like the way Truckerman looked at her. He said all the right things, smiled pleasantly, but his eyes lingered too long on her face and strayed too often to her chest. She pretended not to notice as she drank the bitter coffee. The thick ceramic mug emitted heat and she wrapped her fingers around it to keep them from shaking.

"You look like you could use some rest." Truckerman's voice lowered.

Jules didn't speak. She hid her expression by finishing the hot liquid. It burned the back of her throat, and she coughed lightly.

"This place has a shower and rooms. Nothing fancy, but there's a bed."

Was that hope in his voice? Her empty cup wouldn't afford her refuge again, and the lack of distraction forced her to answer him. "I'm all right." Then, not giving him time to insist she take his offer, she pushed up from the table. Jules grabbed her bag off the floor. "Excuse me a second. I saw a sign for the restrooms."

Jules walked away from the table with no intention of returning. She followed the sign pointing toward the restrooms. Glancing at the table, she saw Truckerman watching her. She forced a quick smile, hoping he didn't try to follow her. Going down a long hall, she kept her eyes averted. The gray-flecked floor tiles matched the drab walls. People had posted notices on a bulletin board, the pages curling from being brushed by passing shoulders—a plea for a lost puppy, a used jet ski for sale, even an ad for masseuse services with a suspiciously dolled up woman in a romantic candlelit setting.

"I wonder what exactly she's offering to massage," Jules muttered.

The hall came to an end, turning in two different directions. One led to showers, beds, and an arcade, the other to the public restrooms. Bells from a pinball machine jingled and clanged. A young boy cheered. Another swore. Jules kept going, looking for an alternate exit. The only one she found had a fire alarm on the door.

Shit!

A row of payphones hung on the wall next to the ladies' room. She thought of Sean's business card in her pocket.

"Leave him out of it," she told herself. "What's he going to do? You're miles from anywhere he'd be."

The faint scent of musky cologne and coconuts wafted over her. She stiffened. The smell triggered her memory, and a flash of pooled blood clouded her vision. Tiny hairs on the back of her neck stood on end, and a chill worked down her spine. How did he find her?

Not daring to turn around, she rushed forward, pushing her palms flat against the restroom door. Smells could linger. He might be gone. It might not be him. Her heart pounded heavy and hard. The door shut behind her as she came face to face with her stricken reflection in the mirror. Her parted lips and pale features looked like a ghost staring back at her. She caught the barest glimpse of a long, dark suit sleeve behind the closing door, obviously belonging to a male by the cut. Tears filled her eyes, and she blinked them back. Frantic, she searched the stalls, knowing by the fall of light she wouldn't find a window hidden behind the metal doors. Nevertheless, she had to try.

A light tap sounded, and she jumped in alarm, startled. Jules dug into her messenger bag for a prepaid cellular phone and hesitated, her thumb hovering over the keypad. She backed away from the door, staring at it. She had no one to call. On instinct, she reached for Sean's card but stopped. No, not Sean. Jules dropped the phone back into the bag. The tapping became louder.

She lifted the strap over her head, letting it hang across her chest to rest on her hip, securing it into place. She searched for a weapon. Someone had bolted everything down, even the base of the trashcan.

Inching toward the door, she threaded her fingers together, braced her feet and waited. The seconds ticked like minutes. Her breath rasped. The door creaked open, too slow to be a woman coming to use the facilities. She lifted her hands to the side like she held an imaginary bat.

"Oh, Jules," a smooth voice sang, the tone low and playful.

Jules didn't wait. She swung before the door even

made it all the way open. Her joined hands met the side of Hector's hard head, slamming it into the metal door. A sharp pain radiated up her wrist and forearm, but she kept moving.

Hector grunted. Jules tried to run past him. He caught her hair and jerked, cursing at her in Spanish. *"Puta, te voy a matar!"*

Hair ripped from her scalp. She wasn't exactly sure how, but she managed to yank free. As she ran around the corner, she saw another human blockade. Truckerman stood, with his arms spread wide to stop her. She quickly got over her surprise as she joined her hands, grunting as she swung for his face. He wasn't as easy to bowl over as Hector had been. Her hands fell short of his head, instead thumping against his shoulder. Truckerman just laughed, grabbing her in a tight bear hug when she tried to run past him. Her back pressed into his chest as she kicked off the floor. An arm blocked her scream. A yellow "wet floor" sign behind him and a cart blocked off the hallway from easy view.

The arcade machines made noise, but no one seemed to be playing them. Her legs flailed in the air. She tried to bite through the thick flannel covering his arm.

Hector's eyes blazed with hate as he faced her.

He slapped at her kicking feet. Jules again tried to bite the arm across her mouth, but her assailant cut off her air, and she struggled for oxygen.

"Easy, sugarplum," Truckerman soothed. "We just want to have a little chat with you."

"*Movete!* Move!" Hector ordered. "Take her to the room. We'll hold her there until tonight when we can transport her. If she gives you any more trouble, do what you have to, but we don't pay for dead. Go. Now."

Jules began to lose consciousness. It took all her energy to keep her eyes open and her vision focused. As he pulled her, Truckerman's arm let up some, and she was able to suck air through her nose.

"Sorry about this, darlin', but you have an enormous reward on your head. I've been out driving the highway hoping to find you." Truckerman's hot breath hit her ear as he whispered. "If not me, someone else would have collected."

Jules's mind raced. He'd been on the phone when he pulled over to pick her up. Had he called Hector? Was the seemingly slow drive a ruse to let Hector catch up? Did he chatter the whole trip to keep her from realizing what he was doing?

Hector's shoes clicked abnormally loud as he led the way down the abandoned hall. She searched for help, but a man like Hector would have covered all angles. No one knew where she was. Help was not coming.

Tears of anger, frustration and fear slipped over her cheeks, hot against her skin. They walked her toward a hall lined with rooms. Stopping at a door marked three, Hector knocked once and was let inside. Truckerman hauled her before him, chuckling as he brought her into her personal hell. Jose and Stewie, two of Hector's associates, stood alongside the door as she was dragged past. A fast *pfft* sounded behind her, and a fine mist sprayed across her shoulder and arm, over the floor to concentrate on the wall. Truckerman's hold slackened, and his weight pressed into her. Jules gasped in shock, stumbling toward a small bed on the far side of the tiny room to keep from being trampled.

Her knee hit the hard floor, sending a jolt of pain up her hip. She grabbed the mattress for support. As she endeavored to stand, she saw blood spatter dotted the wall. Shaking, she forced herself to turn. Stewie was in the process of sheathing his weapon. He'd shot Truckerman, without hesitation or warning. The dead body took up a good portion of the floor space.

"Move him," Hector ordered. Jose and Stewie grabbed Truckerman and slid him to rest against the wall, shoving him over as far as they could. Lifeless eyes stared at them, no longer bearing witness to their deeds. Hector saw her looking and walked over to the body. He nudged the dead man's jaw with the tip of his boot to make it look as if Truckerman spoke in a terrible Southern accent, "Don't ya worry, darlin'. They just want to talk to ya. Now where is my money? I want my money." He laughed at his own morbid joke before telling the corpse, "You have your reward, trucker."

Deliberately, dark eyes turned from Truckerman to her. Hector grinned. A red splotch marred the side of his head where she'd struck him. And on the opposite side a darker spot where he'd hit the restroom door.

"You've been hard to find," he said.

"Sorry," Jules answered with mock bravado to hide her deep fear. "Didn't mean to put you out. Felt the need to get out of the city."

"The way I see it, you have two options." Hector dominated the room with his stance though he was the shortest of them all. His legs spread wide, and he crossed his arms over his chest. "One, you tell me who you told our little secret to and maybe I believe you and maybe I don't kill everyone you know. You die fast. Two, you keep your mouth shut, I kill everyone you know while you watch, but you get to die slow with the knowledge you didn't rat on your friends. Either way, I will kill you, and I will get the recording before I do."

Jules screamed. What did she have to lose? Hector instantly stepped forward, slapping her across the jaw with the back of his hand. The acrid flavor of blood filled her mouth. Her body flung to the side, and she fell on the bed. Her knee jarred again, this time on the mattress. The padding didn't help. She held onto the injured limb, whimpering.

"Try that again, *princesa*, and I'll assume you chose option two," Hector warned. "Everyone you've ever looked at will end up an ice cube floating in a morgue martini. No one's coming to save you, Jules. *Comprendes?*"

Hector swiped a thumb across her mouth. Stewie chuckled.

"I said, do you understand?" Hector yelled.

Jules jolted at the harsh sound before nodding once. Playing it stupid would not help her get out of there. She'd have to wait and watch and pray for a way to escape. "Yeah, Hector, I understand you perfectly."

THE IDEA of Jules and the trucker burned into Sean's mind, filling him with jealousy. How could she think of another man after they'd been together? Every fiber of his being knew she belonged with him. And, yet, he'd watched as she walked to the restrooms, giving one last lingering smile at the man she was with. The trucker made what appeared to be a text message on his cellular, threw cash down on the table, glanced around like a boy about to receive his first real sword and followed Jules. Sean waited for the man to come back. He didn't. Seconds ticked on, each plucking at his soul like a razorblade. Is this how she paid for her rides?

He tried to act inconspicuous by wandering through the store section, but his eyes kept straying toward the restrooms. A blockade had been set up so a janitor could mop the floors. Sean fingered a candy bar, tapping it against the palm of his hand in agitation. He tried to listen down the hall for Jules, but an unseen worker ran some kind of machine that made a loud grinding noise. Tracking her would be so much easier if he were on his home planet. His hand twitched, and he realized he was crushing the candy.

"Sir, can I help you?" A young cashier looked at him. Her hands thrust into the pockets of her black uniform apron. She tilted her head to the side, the long length of her brunette ponytail swinging to and fro.

"Does the janitor normally clean this time of day?" He asked, tossing the warped candy bar back onto the shelf.

"I don't think so. He comes in during the early morning hours unless some kid puked in the bathrooms again," she answered with a shrug. "Why? You need to go? Just head on back. You won't get in trouble. That caution sign isn't a law or anything. No one cares if you walk on the wet floor."

"What about the rooms you rent to truckers? Who does that?" Sean fought the sick feeling in his stomach.

"Oh, you want a room? I do that up here at the

register, but you have to be a trucker. Are you a trucker?" She had a small bounce in her step as she disappeared behind the sales counter to grab a ledger.

"Yes." Sean nodded.

"Great," her bubbly voice answered. "Fifty bucks will get you a room for the rest of the afternoon and evening and a shower. Plus, you get ten percent off any beverage purchase."

"What rooms are taken, um," Sean glanced at her nametag, "Sharon."

"Uh," Sharon looked confused, even as she looked at her ledger. "Just room three and six. Actually, six will be open in an hour. Some lady trucker checked in late last night and has a wake-up call scheduled. Why? You superstitious and need a certain room number?"

"Give me room one," Sean said, digging out his wallet. He threw a fifty on the table. The cashier never asked for an ID or proof he drove a semi, just slid a paper over for him to sign.

Sharon glanced down at the paper, handed over a key with the number "one" written on the side with permanent marker, smiled and said, "Thanks, Mr. Smith."

JULES HAD no idea how much time passed between Hector's talking, the lifeless eyes of the trucker's corpse staring at her, the leer of Hector's goons, and the frantic beat of her heart resounding in her ears. Each measured second stretched, pulsing with fear and adrenaline. Her knee throbbed, and she knew she couldn't run very fast. She wouldn't have to make it far. If she could just escape the room, she might make it to the restaurant, to public, to safety.

The side of her head pulsated from where she'd been struck, payback from having hit Hector as she ran out of the restroom. Her stiff neck was a present from Truckerman's rough handling. The nausea could be blamed on any of her captors.

The fact no one heard or saw her abduction

didn't surprise her. People were unaware by nature and without a loud gunshot to jolt them from their comfortable lives they wouldn't pay any attention to some behind-the-wet-floor-sign struggle beyond their small universes. The noise would be drowned out in a sea of conversation, clanking silverware, deafening arcade machines and truck stop staff busily at work. She'd seen it happen plenty of times. Once, she'd gotten into a fight with a prostitute in an alley behind a bar. Even with all the crashing and irate screams, no one from the passing sidewalk came to investigate. The bitch had shoved her into a pile of fluorescent light bulbs leaning against a dumpster. It took hours to wash the glassy powder out of her hair.

Snapping fingers drew her wandering mind back to the present. This situation was much, much worse. A cold chill worked over her, despite the hot room. The contents of her messenger bag were strewn around the bed from Stewie rummaging through her belongings. They'd searched her for a wire, leaving her shirt torn and her bra exposed. The fact amused her—like she intended to set them up with her elaborate plan of running away and going into hiding.

Jules swung her knees to the side, pressing them tightly together beneath the skirt. The sensation of their hands on her, touching and searching, was much like what she imagined swarming roaches would feel like on her flesh. Stewie's widening grin as he stared at her torn shirt irritated her, and she wished to scratch the expression from his ugly face.

"Who did you tell?" Hector asked, standing beside her.

"Oh, good, the interrogation part." Jules gave a derisive laugh. She would never give him the satisfaction of crying and pleading. Tears didn't sway men like Hector, but rather they were empowered by them. "I thought I was going to have to listen to you talk all day."

"You know, Jules." Hector laughed, pointing his finger at her. "I like you."

"Well, I'm not looking for a relationship right now," she quipped, "but thanks for thinking of me."

His laughter grew. He turned to his men. "She is a very funny lady."

"You want me to tell her a few jokes, boss?" Jose asked, menacingly.

"No." Hector gently touched her face. "I want to take her back to the city. *Vamos a ver como le gusta a la señora ser una prostitute?*"

The men laughed. Stewie's leer only deepened.

"*Besa mi culo.* I will never be your whore," Jules

swore, moving to stand. Glaring at him, she hissed, "*Andate al infierno.*"

"You," he pointed at her, hesitating as if surprised she understood what he had been saying, "tell me to go to hell? I own hell, *maldita puta.* I am the devil. When I get done pumping your veins full of *heroína,* you'll do whatever I tell you, *who*ever I tell you."

She opened her mouth to retort, but a loud crash interrupted her. The lock on the door busted, and the wood splintered. Jules automatically lifted her arms to protect her face. By the time the debris quit hitting her legs, and she'd lowered her arms, Stewie lay on the floor, and a blurry image swung at Jose. Jules didn't think, just acted. She leaped toward a surprised Hector, ramming her shoulder into his chest to knock him over. Her knee bumped his legs, and she cried out as the pain caused her to stumble awkwardly. A steady hand caught her from behind. She turned to her rescuer, only to come face to face with an otherworldly creature. Dark brown skin covered his face with a hard shell. The forehead, nose, and brow formed a protective ridge over his yellow, reptilian eyes. He was part man, part dragon, and there was something familiar about him. Before she could speak, he flung her toward the door to safety.

As her back hit against the frame, she gasped for breath. The two men on the floor bled at the temples and didn't move. The dragon creature had Hector pressed against the wall by his throat. Only, it wasn't a creature. It was Sean. She recognized him by the stance of his body, and the breadth of his shoulders. He drew his fist back. Hector smirked as if he hadn't a care in the world.

"Nice mask," Hector mocked. "Is that supposed to scare me, lizard boy?"

"Sean," Jules whispered, confused. She felt her head to see if she'd bumped it. Was this a full-blown delusion? Or had she indeed seen the dragon man come to her rescue? "Sean?"

Wait, no. Hector saw it, too. Only he assumed it was a mask.

Sean's weight shifted. Talons grew from the tips of his fingers. She couldn't let him stab Hector. Even if the scumbag deserved it, she wouldn't let Sean commit murder over her. "Sean, you can't."

Sean's hand tensed, and his knuckles turned white.

"You better listen to her, Sean," Hector taunted, clearly not seeing the razor blades growing from Sean's fingers. "This has nothing to do with you."

Sean growled. Like a striking snake, his hand shot

forward. The talons retracted seconds before he struck the side of Hector's head just behind his temple. The man crumpled, the smirk still lingering on his features.

Relief filled her as Sean rushed across the room, maneuvering over three unconscious men and a corpse. The dragon mask molded into human flesh as he came for her. Within seconds, all traces of his alter ego had disappeared.

"Sean," Jules tried to reason what she was seeing.

"Did you touch anything?" he asked. "Brian taught me about prints."

Jules glanced around, unable to remember. She lifted her hands toward the bed. "Yes?"

"Where?"

"Yes," she mumbled again, staring at his face.

"Jules, sweetheart, did they touch you?" His eyes went to her torn shirt. "Did they—?"

"You..." She lifted her shaky hand to point at his face.

"Jules, try to concentrate. Did they harm you?" His finger brushed over the side of her face where Hector had struck her.

The sting of her bruise woke her from her daze. "No, no, they just tried to scare me."

"We need to leave."

Jules nodded in understanding. She rushed to the bed, shoving her belongings into the messenger bag.

"We have to wipe for prints." Sean reached into his pocket to search for something to clean up her fingerprints.

"There isn't time." She tugged on his arm. "The door's busted. We can't chance them waking up. More of Hector's men could be on their way. We have to go now. Hector will undoubtedly take care of the evidence if the authorities don't find him passed out next to a dead body."

Sean looked like he wanted to argue, but let her pull him out of the room. The hall was empty, and Jules thanked her lucky stars for small favors.

"Here." He shrugged out of his leather jacket. "Put this on."

She did, slipping her arms through the sleeves as they walked. His warmth and scent surrounded her and made her feel safe. Tugging the front together, she hid her bloodstained shirt. Jules glanced behind them to make sure they weren't being followed. She grabbed the wet floor sign and pulled it a few feet back to block the hallway leading to the rooms, making sure to pick it up with the leather coat between her skin and the plastic. It wouldn't do to get her prints on anything else. With any luck, the room would be so dirty from guests they wouldn't be able to find hers.

Sean stopped her before they reached the store area, making her look at him. Serious eyes moved over her features as he pulled his fingers through her hair, straightening the locks. She flinched as he bumped the bruise on her face and leaned back to look at his fingers. They appeared human.

"I can explain later, but for now, I need you to know that I won't hurt you," he whispered. Jules hesitated and then nodded. She was more frightened of Hector than of Sean's whatever-it-was. Slipping his arm around her shoulders, he led her down the hall to the restaurant section.

"Keep your head by my chest." He pulled her against him. Her hair fell over her cheeks, hiding the side of her face. The warmth of him spread through her. He laughed and his voice became louder than before, as he said for the benefit of anyone listening, "I already told you, sweetheart, we won't be in New York for a few more days, but I promise you, you can do your shopping then."

She glanced up at him with a wry look, arched a brow, but said nothing. He walked her outside, keeping their pace slow, but not too slow. She couldn't help the relief she felt as she took a deep breath of fresh air. Jules hated to admit how scared she'd been and how glad she was that Sean came to her rescue.

"So, shopping?" she asked.

"It is a lady thing to do, right?" he answered. "I was trying to act casual. You have blood on your face and ripped clothing."

The thought of Truckerman's blood on her skin caused her to stiffen. "Where are we going?"

"Where I should have made you go three days ago," he answered, walking faster. "Hell, where I should have made you go two years ago. I'm taking you home with me."

"WHAT WERE YOU THINKING, JULES?" Sean had kept his curiosity at bay as they journeyed down the interstate in the old pickup truck, navigating through the heavy traffic around Baltimore. They'd passed over the Patapsco River and along parts of the Chesapeake Bay, able to see the gorgeous views of the water from the road before turning inland. She'd cleaned her face with a bottle of water and put on one of his extra t-shirts. It would be nearly seven hours before they arrived in Boston. "I know you saw me change."

"Can't we keep driving in silence?" She turned her eyes from where they'd been fixed alongside the road. Evening darkened the sky, casting gentle shadows over her face. When she looked at him, his chest tightened. His body knew her. Every nerve reached to bring her closer, his heart ached with the dull, broken pain only that organ could produce. But, how could someone be so familiar and such a stranger? No matter how much he needed her, he would not force himself on her, especially now that the dragon inside him had scared her. She kept her gaze focused on his face. "I know how to handle the silence."

Sean shook his head in denial. He wanted to reach for her and take her hand in his, but it didn't appear like she wanted his comfort. Looking at her and not being able to hold her only intensified his loneliness.

"I can explain." Sean gripped the steering wheel tight. He needed to tell her.

"You can explain how you changed forms into some supernatural lizard?" Jules gave a small, humorless laugh. "I'm just happy I'm not crazy. When you rescued me the first time, I thought I saw...something. Detective Flaherty convinced me I was insane after the blow to my head. But it seemed real, as real as the memory of my mother's face. And so I was convinced I had brain damage. I had dreams about it. My mind was obsessed with it. I read romance novels about it. Now I know it was you. I'm not crazy. You're a supernatural lizard."

"I'm a dragon-shifter from another planet. Not a supernatural lizard something."

"Dragon-shifter alien."

"I don't know that I am an alien, not like the Reticulans are aliens. I came here through a portal from another planet on the night we first met, but my people left Earth long ago through that same portal. The night we met was our first trip back in centuries."

"Centuries," she repeated.

"We are called the Draig. Maybe you've heard of us?" Sean asked, his tone almost hopeful. He often wondered if any of his kind had been left behind on the planet when their elders first moved to Qurilixen. What if they were in hiding?

"Draig? No."

"How about the Var? Cat-shifters? They came with us through the portals too."

"Cat-shifters? No." She shook her head in slow denial and kept staring at him with a strange look on her face.

"Are you...?" He glanced at her in worry.

"In shock?" she finished. "Not really. I'm just listening, taking it all in. Please go on."

"We were not expecting humans to be so," he

paused, tapping the wheel as he drove, "so how you are."

"You sound like you're from here," she said. "More so than when I came to visit you after my attack."

"Duncan taught me to blend. He said I am a quick study."

"Ah, yes, Detective Flaherty."

"The Flaherty family has been good to me. They have taken me in and shown me the ways of your kind. Had they not intervened, I would be living as a wild man in the forest." Sean gave her a meaningful look. "When I first came to your planet, I didn't know who to trust. I wasn't supposed to stay, or reveal myself, or even interact if it could be avoided. My rulers made that very clear. I heard you scream and then...well, you know the rest. Duncan saw what I was, and since I saved Brian while saving you, they returned the favor. They took me in. They fed me. They taught me how to blend. Duncan secured papers to make me appear as if I belonged on this planet and let me use the family name. They shortened Seanan of the Draig to Sean Flaherty. If no one looks too closely at my background, I should remain safe. Fillan Flaherty helped me buy a place to live. Rory Flaherty taught me how to battle Earth-style without shifting with DVD movie tutorials. Brian helped me to register as a bounty hunter with the Boston Earth governing authority and to make contact with local bail bondsmen, who in turn hire me as an independent hunter. They don't ask questions because I always bring in the bad guys."

"Whoa, ah, Sean, watch the road." Jules braced her hand against the dashboard. He realized he'd been staring at her intently instead of watching where he was steering and quickly corrected the truck's course off the interstate's shoulder.

"I apologize. I was raised riding ceffyls and they don't require as much direction as your vehicles."

"Do ceffyls walk slow?"

He frowned and nodded. "They keep a steady pace. Why?"

Jules gave a tired laugh. "Because you drive slower than a grandma with night blindness."

"I drive at the pace set by your governing rulers." He pointed to the dashboard and then a passing road sign to show her the speed matched.

"So you were saying? Dragon-shifter universal traveler to Earth bounty hunter," she prompted. "I can understand why the bail bondsmen turn a blind eye to you, but what about the police? Or the courts?

Don't you have to go to trial about your line of work at all?"

"Since the Flaherty clan is comprised mostly of police officers spread out over the state, I simply notified them when I am hunting in their territory. As long as I bring the bad guys in, no one seems to care. If anyone digs, they will find I have no real Earth documentation, so I am careful not to raise suspicion. Until you, Duncan's immediate family members were the only ones who knew my secret. Since Duncan vouched for me, the other clan members don't question how I track more criminals than any other hunter out there."

"You might not want to call them clan members," Jules inserted. "Just an Earth tip."

"Thank you," he answered. "As you see I am still learning, even though I have assimilated."

"So dragon-shifter, part alien, bounty hunter, Sean Flaherty."

"I would like for you to consider me your lover as well." Sean smiled, happy that he was finally able to speak the request out loud to her. In truth, he wanted to be more than her lover. He wanted to mate her and someday do the Earth binding ceremony.

Jules bit her lip and hid her face from him as she

looked out the window. "Let's see where the night takes us."

Sean grinned and shifted uncomfortably in his seat, his arousal heavy and begging for attention. He knew where he'd like the night to take them. Was it unromantic to pulled over to the side of the road? He cleared his throat and forced himself to focus on driving in a straight line. "Since you are not alarmed by my shifting, I believe it is your turn to speak. Why did those men kidnap you and rip your clothing?"

"I'll make you a deal. You find a place to pull over for the night, and we'll talk." Jules made a show of yawning. "I feel like I've been awake for a month and this truck's shocks bounce. It's making me carsick."

"Deal." He didn't hide the eagerness from his tone. Seeing a sign for a hotel, he eased off the inter-state, not bothering to note what town they were in. He kept his attention focused on her though he tried not to show it. "Now speak as I find a place. Why is the Velázquez crime family after you?"

"Wrong place, wrong time," she answered.

"You seem to have been in that position quite a bit over the last few years."

"You checked up on me?" Jules's tone dropped to a low whisper.

"I was concerned about you. Don't be mad. I had

Brian use his connections to check on you so I could monitor what you have been doing for the past two years, but not to stalk you. Stalking isn't good. I hunted a stalker. He was...not good."

"So that's how you tracked me?"

"I hunted you. Like a bond, but a good bond, one who I'm not going to take to jail."

"No offense to you or Brian and his cop family, but the law isn't putting those who deserve it in jail. Someone needed to keep an eye on things. That's all I do. I watch, I listen, and I report. Sometimes things get a little rough. Sometimes a car is stolen." She sighed, her words coming faster, like a conversation she'd had a hundred times. "Cops catch them. But, without evidence, the courts have to let them go. Witnesses are too scared to come forward against the worst offenders. Those criminals not immediately released on their own recognizance are taken out by bail bondsmen. It's a broken system."

Suddenly, she stopped, and he felt her eyes boring into him. Tension rolled down his neck and back. He'd expected her to be upset about his heritage. That seemed reasonable. Instead, she was mad about his Earth job. What else was he supposed to do? On his home world he followed the orders of his king and queen for the betterment of his people.

Here, he chased after those who the human law told him needed to go back to jail.

"How can you do it, Sean?" She took off her seatbelt to better turn toward him. "I saw the men in your files. How can you be part of the system that lets them out?"

"Because I can track them," Sean defended. "I did not invent the rules of your society. Someone will post bail. I know I can keep tabs on them. And, working for a bondsman, when they skip court I get more leeway with the methods in which I bring them in. In that situation, I can do more than the police." He turned the truck, parking alongside the front entrance. "I haven't let one get away yet."

He refused to think about his current prey, Dougie. At least Dougie wouldn't do anything violent. The man was more destructive to himself than to society. Most likely, after he showed at court, he'd be given a reduced sentence for any information he could supply to help catch a bigger criminal. Brian told him that the higher bond amount was just a scare tactic used by the District Attorney to get Dougie squealing, and to discover if he was connected enough to have anyone cover the amount for him. Dougie wasn't. His mother ended up bailing him out, putting her home and family business up as collateral.

"What job would you have me do?" Sean asked. "I am not qualified for much here. What I have is the ability to see through your darkness and listen past what humans can hear. I can hunt. I can fight. I can track. That is what I can do. I did not wish for this life, but it is the risk I accepted when I stepped through the portal."

"I'm tired," she said. He could tell by her tone she didn't want to talk anymore, not that she'd said too much to begin with.

"Promise me you'll wait here," he ordered. "This conversation isn't over."

Blue eyes met his, and she nodded once. "I'm too tired to run away, and I need a shower."

14

Each heavy, sliding footstep led Jules closer to sleep. As she moved over the room's threshold, her eyes strayed to the one queen-size bed in the middle of the room. Her pace didn't falter.

"They did not have rooms with two beds left." Sean almost sounded apologetic. Almost.

"Good." The knowledge of where she'd be right now if not for his rescue filled her. He'd saved her. Again. Was her desire for him gratitude? It didn't feel like simple gratitude. The need to touch him burned beneath her skin, zapping her flesh like bolts of internal lightning fighting to break free.

In the truck, she knew the conversation he wanted to have. But, Jules didn't want to talk about her life. As she neared the bed, she could think of several things she'd much rather do and sleep no longer appeared so important. She dropped her bag on the floor before slipping out of his oversized t-shirt. Next, she kicked off her shoes. Fingers slid down her naked arm, and she felt the warmth of him along her back.

"Are you sure they didn't hurt you?" Sean asked, his voice soft.

Jules turned only to meet with his chest. Everything about him appeared human. The scent of his cologne curled around her senses. He always smelled great. Her eyes traveled up, slow and steady over strong muscles. Bronzed cords led in thick lines to his stiff jaw. The textured shadow of facial hair mingled with the smoothness of flesh. Every line seemed so perfect—a firmly sculpted mouth, the divot above his lip, straight nose with a small bump at the bridge where it had healed from being broken. "You don't look like a dragon."

His eyes flashed with yellow, shifting only to return to normal once more.

"I saw you that night. I knew I saw you," she whispered.

"You didn't answer. Are you sure they did not hurt you?" The serious look in his eyes pierced into her with his worry.

Jules shook her head in denial. "No. Not like that. Although, I would like a shower."

"I'll, ah..." Sean glanced at her mouth. "I'll start the water for you."

She expected him to kiss her, but he withdrew quickly, his movements awkward and jerking as he went to turn on the shower. Why the sudden shyness? She would've laughed if her body didn't ache to feel him inside her once more. The sound of running water drew her attention, and she found herself pursuing him.

Sean withdrew his wet hand from beneath the stream of water. "It'll take a second to warm—"

Jules grabbed his shirt and pulled him to her so hard their mouths bumped together, causing her teeth to press against the sensitive inside of her bottom lip. She didn't care. Sean made a weak noise of surprise before opening his mouth. Passion sizzled between them, burning in each rip of clothing, each thrust of the tongue, each loud groan.

Mindless, she freed him of his clothes, eager to run her hands over his taut flesh. In their urgency, they stumbled against the shower curtain. The unsecured hold of plastic caused them to part long enough to step into the cool water. Jules gasped at the chilly shock.

Sean shut the curtain. She pressed into his heat, warming against him as she rubbed her full length to his. The push of his arousal against her stomach grew at the intimate contact. They enjoyed the glide of wet flesh and, by small degrees, the water heated. Droplets pounded her side, splashing up on her face to moisten her lips. She kissed him, trapping him against the shower stall. Her hands roamed over his chest and shoulders. He trembled in response, touching her wherever he could reach—massaging her arms, running fingers over her back, cupping her ass so hard her heels lifted off the tub floor.

Jules wanted to devour him. She licked his jaw, biting her way to his earlobe. Sean made small animalistic noises in the back of his throat, spurring her on. She ran her hand lightly over his flat stomach and thighs until his body squirmed. Forging a trail with the tip of her tongue, she traced the flow of muscle down his chest, pausing only to tease each small, erect nipple.

The water flow hit her directly on the side of the face, so she turned her back to it, sliding him roughly along the slick wall. Sean braced himself as Jules aggressively kissed his stomach. His harsh breath echoed overhead. Jules grinned, liking the idea of control in an otherwise erratic world.

His erection stood tall from his narrow hips. The thick shaft was long enough to please without being too much. As her mouth moved along his hipbone, he jerked. His groans became louder. His fingers delved into her hair, urging her mouth lower. Her feet met with the textured skid proof surface of the tub. She grasped his hips and darted her tongue over his shaft. A small sound of pleasure escaped her lips before she enveloped him. She sucked him into her mouth and brought her hands to stroke the extra length.

Jules loved the sound of his sharp breaths as she grazed him with her teeth. His hands gripped her hair, pushing deep into her mouth, as the water cocooned her in its beating warmth. She continued her caresses, drawing out his pleasure. His hips thrust to keep the rhythm she set. She cupped his balls, rolling them gently before venturing to the hidden stretch of flesh beneath the soft globes.

Soon, it wasn't enough to control him. Jules slithered up his body. Sean swung her around, switching their positions in the shower. She held onto his shoulders as he pinned her to the wall.

"Jules, I..." He tried to speak, but she pursed her lips, stopping him.

Sean's legs threaded between hers, parting them. He lifted her up, holding her firmly by the thighs.

She supported herself by grabbing his shoulders. Urgently, she wrapped her legs around his waist, and hooked her ankles behind him, guiding him forward. Their bodies met. Anticipation built, causing her thighs to contract.

Sean guided himself to her opening. He entered her hard. Jules sucked in a long, rasping breath. Her muscles stretched, fitting perfectly around him. Whimpering, she closed her eyes—feeling every sensation, hearing every noise. She met his thrusts the best she could in their position.

Jules let go of reason, unable to think as the demand for release filled every ounce of her body. A tremor worked over them, and he increased his pace. Her thoughts couldn't focus beyond the grunt of his voice, the stroke of his arousal, the brush of his mouth against her cheek.

The tension between them heightened to a feverish pitch. She didn't want it to end, but she couldn't fight her climax. Her nails dug into his shoulders. Release surged over her, erupting from between her thighs to spread out over her body. He jerked, grunting loud and long as he came. Jules's legs slid down to the tub floor, but her bones felt as if they'd melted.

"I'll get you soap so you may finish your shower."

He breathed hard, his hands lingering before letting go. "You said you needed sleep."

Sean stepped out of the shower, and Jules gave in to gravity, sitting so that the water hit her body like rain. She heard him leave the bathroom. Her lips barely moved, as she whispered, "Thank you for saving me again, Sean."

15

"I LOOKED for you after you disappeared," Sean said, his voice quiet. Warm hands ran along her naked spine. Jules sighed, not wanting to move from the middle of the hotel bed. Sean's body stretched next to hers, and she traced small circles along his back.

"I needed time to think. I hitchhiked around a few states." Jules blinked hard, trying to keep her eyes open. The stress of the last several days combined with the sleepy heat of his body made it hard.

"I didn't mean now. I meant then." He continued to caress her in leisurely, comforting movements. "When I first arrived here, after I healed from the gunshot, I looked for you."

"I know what you meant. I hoped you'd let it

slide." Jules let her hand drop onto the bed to rest next to him. "I didn't want to be found. After you had saved me, I felt so much. Duncan convinced me it was victim bonding. He said it happened all the time. You rescued me from a horrible thing, and in return, I distorted who I was and who you were to me. That kind of love isn't real. It also didn't help that I had doubts about why the Flahertys were in the alleyway that night. What are the odds off duty cops would be walking by at the same time three criminals were having a secret meeting?"

"You believed the Flahertys were corrupt? So you thought I was corrupt, as well, because I was there? Do you still think that way?" The sadness in his voice struck her, filling her with a deep and dismal pain in the center of her chest.

"I wondered about it for a time. Though, to be fair, I hated everyone and everything, and trusted no one." Jules didn't want to think about the past. She'd spent years burying it. "At first, I was so confused and angry, but then I went numb, and by that time there was no point in going back. So much had happened. With my mom dead, I had no family to go to, so I decided to start over. Everything I had was gone."

"I was there. What I felt the moment I saw you wasn't confused. I still feel it."

Jules sighed. "Life as I lived it died that night."

She closed her eyes, remembering the sound of rain on wet concrete. It had dripped in slow, fat drops, sliding over storefront windows illuminated by yellow streetlights. A chill gripped the city, despite the early fall season. She'd worn her favorite gray knit sweater.

"Jules?" Sean interrupted her thoughts.

"Can I see you do it?" Jules pulled her hand slightly away from his chest but didn't get up.

"You want to see me change?"

Jules nodded. "Yes." She focused on keeping her tone calm and her expression blank. The dim light coming through the narrow part in the curtain gave little to see by, but her eyes had adjusted to the darkness.

He kept touching her, the stroke of his hands hypnotic against her skin. First, his eyes shifted to gold. The flesh over the bridge of his nose darkened and grew, forming a ridge over his brow. Brown armor spread over his face and down his neck.

Jules's breathing deepened. Her fingers shook as she reached to touch his cheek. The texture of his skin was exactly how she imagined a medieval beast might feel though he looked more like a hybrid man-dragon.

His lips parted to reveal fangs, and a low growl sounded in the back of his throat. The fingertips against her arm turned into talons but stroked her as lightly as before. Unable to help herself, she leaned back and glanced down the length of his body. The armor continued lower to cover his cock.

"I'm not scared of you," she whispered. His features softened once more to the Sean she knew.

"You shouldn't be. I would never hurt you. I stayed here because of you. I would do anything to protect you."

"You left your home world. You gave up so much, and I can't even remember if I said thank you."

"You don't need to thank me."

"We never really talked about what happened that night." She scratched the side of her neck. "I should have found a ride home, but my mother had just died after a long battle with cancer, and I had no one to help me through it. I felt like my lungs were collapsing inside my chest. I couldn't breathe. Every-thing hurt." Jules closed her eyes, each detail of what happened still vivid.

"I am sorry about your mother. It is never easy to lose someone in a fight."

"It was a fight against an illness," she said. "Not an actual battle."

"Again, I am saddened to hear it."

"Thank you." She nodded in appreciation before continuing her story. "Bruiser McManus bonded out Sammy Boy, Frankie and Joey. They were up on murder charges, but the authorities were still trying to make their case at that point."

"That case is how Duncan first explained the way bonds worked to me. I wanted to hunt them down and kill them. He would not let me."

"Bruiser was an imbecile. He'd bond out anyone with enough cash and barely bothered chasing them if they ran. It's no wonder he's out of business. Those three jumped bail weeks before, and he spent more time questioning people in bars than out on the streets looking for them."

"If the man hadn't quit, he would've been scared out of Boston. I would have seen to it. The worst offenders I track the moment I hear about their case, even before they officially jump bond." Sean didn't stop touching her. His hand moved over her hip, the full palm pressing to her flesh. "Men like Sammy Boy, Frankie and Joey will not have the chance to hurt more people. Not on my watch."

"It's not like they were waiting for me. I walked

by the wrong alley at the wrong time." Jules had a feeling he knew most of what had happened to her, more or less, but he didn't know everything. "I heard Frankie say something to Joey, using his name. I glanced over at the sound. They saw me, and Sammy Boy panicked. I ran, but the sidewalks were uneven, and I had those stupid heels on. I tripped in a puddle and fell. Two of them grabbed my legs and dragged me into the alley behind a dumpster." She fought to keep her tone even, still unable to look at him directly. "I remember trying to grab the sidewalk, but the concrete scratched my face and hands, and I couldn't get a good grip on anything."

"Jules, you don't have to give details if it's too painful." He stroked her cheek.

"No, I owe you the story." She paused, half expecting him to insist it wasn't necessary. He didn't. Jules swallowed nervously. "As you know, they beat me pretty badly and would have left me for dead if not for you. The strange thing is, when I was lying there on the ground, their boots slamming into my body, I remember staring at the side of that green dumpster, covered in yellow graffiti, 'Bobby loves Janet'. I dream about it sometimes, that dumpster."

Sean ran his thumb along the edge of her bottom lip. He watched her mouth as she spoke.

"I tried to fight and managed to break Joey's necklace. Then you came. In one moment you were there, like an angel that flew in from above to save me."

"I don't fly. I am a dragon-shifter. Not a full blood. I don't even know if full bloods exist anymore."

"You're my angel. You came, and you stopped them from killing me." Jules moved her hand down his stomach. "You took the bullet meant for me." She traced a line from one old scar to another. "And then the bullet that was meant for Brian when he and Duncan came to help, drunk from their evening celebrating at the cop bar. You scared the evil away. When I woke up in the hospital, I thought you'd be there. No one knew anything about a man with two gunshot wounds."

"Brian and Duncan saw me shift. They knew your government wouldn't let something like me be, so they took me to a private street doctor. He fixed me up the best he could, and I healed on my own. Duncan said he owed me for his son's life. For that he would protect me like I was family." Sean cupped her cheek. "Why did you leave? I wanted to find you, but I didn't know how. Everything was so chaotic and new."

"You didn't ask me to stay when I came to thank you. In fact, you didn't say much at all."

"I didn't know how. Earth language had changed so much."

"You could have asked in other ways." Jules brushed her mouth against his.

"You didn't give me permission. Aside from traveling ships, you were the first unmarried woman I'd talked to. What right did I have to ask? I had nothing. No home. No way to get back to my family, to my planet, to a place where I could provide for you."

"They told me I didn't see what I saw. Duncan said I was traumatized. You weren't some supernatural being come to save me. You were just a man who did the right thing." Jules pulled away, as she tried to distance her emotions. His hands slipped from her body.

Sean didn't answer. Jules made herself face him. He sat on the bed. A sheet covered his waist but left his chest bare. Shadows fell across his features, making them impossible to read.

"They said if it weren't for you, I would be dead, and that is why I thought I liked you."

"Duncan told you to leave me?" The whisper seemed to fill the room.

"No. Yes. Kind of."

"He must have been trying to protect me from discovery." Sean pushed up from the bed, each movement stiff and deliberate. "It's different now."

"How? I get into trouble, and you come to save me again just like last time. How do I know what I'm feeling isn't just more hero worship? I'm a romanticized damsel in distress, and you're the dragon man who comes to save me."

"I am a man, and you are a woman. It would make sense that I protect you. I will take care of you. I have means now. I have work. I have a home in Southie. You shall live with me, and I will keep you safe. I—"

"Sean, stop. I didn't—*don't* want to be taken care of! I can take care of myself."

"Is that what all this is?" His voice rose as he swept his arm over the hotel room. "You taking care of yourself?"

She stiffened. He had a point. She was on the run from a crime family, and if he stayed with her, he'd be on the run too. "I don't want to talk anymore. What we have is chemistry, simple sexual attraction. Don't mistake that for anything more. We're just two people whose paths have crossed a couple of times."

"Fine." Sean went for his suitcase and then pulled on a pair of jeans. "Get some rest. Don't try to run. I can track you." He didn't look at her as he turned toward the door.

"Sean, I..." Jules wasn't sure what she should say.

"Get some sleep. I'll be back."

"Sean," she tried again.

"I dislike these words you are saying. I need to go for a walk." He held up his hand to stop her from speaking and strode barefoot to the door. It slammed shut behind him.

Not knowing what else to do, Jules crawled onto the bed and pulled the covers tight around her body. She rolled onto her back and rubbed her temples. This was the way it had to be. She couldn't ruin his life by being a part of it. A cold emptiness surrounded her, but part of her still hoped Sean would come back into the room, hold her in his arms and tell her everything would be all right. He didn't, and she was left alone more confused than before.

How HAD life come to this? Sean felt lost on a strange path, far away from where he should be. Once, he understood exactly what his life was. He'd been a palace guard, like many in his family before him. He worked, maintained the family honor, hunted, rode ceffyls, shifted in the forest, camped with his brother, and prayed to his gods that one day he'd help to secure his people's future by bringing potential brides through a portal.

A hard knot formed in the pit of his stomach as he looked up at the sky. He missed home. He missed his brother. He missed being around other shifters whose ways made sense. Honor was important. Duty must be done. Mates were for life. Love was not questioned.

How the fuck did this happen? One miserable night. One miserably unlucky forsaken night. He had accepted that he might die when he volunteered to be the first from his generation to step across the universe. No one could guess what Earth would be like after centuries of his people being away. Death in service to his dragon-shifter kind was a reasonable risk. Even dying to protect a strange human woman was reasonable. What wasn't reasonable was finding the one woman in all the universes he should be with and realizing she didn't want him back. It broke his heart. The pain was worse than death. There was nothing he could do. His dragon had bonded to the woman, and there would never be another.

"I can't believe you found Jules. It's so romantic the way you saved her, and then lost her, and now found her again. Is she coming home?" Teresa Flaherty had him on speakerphone.

Sean's hand twitched, and he nearly crushed the device. Apparently, Brian had called everyone else in his immediate family to tell them what was going on.

"It's about time you got a girlfriend." Fillan was evidently there, too. He was the second oldest of the four Flaherty brothers and the only one who'd married.

"It's not Sean's fault," the youngest brother, Rory

defended, before teasing, "that he's a loser with the ladies."

A loud smacking noise sounded followed by Rory's cry of protest and their father's gruff words of warning.

"Brian had told us about Hector. Don't worry. We're all keeping a close eye on his crew," Duncan said. "He won't make a move in this city without a cop on his tail."

"He's not in the city," Sean said. Then, not wanting to scare Teresa, he added, "Duncan, take me off the speaker."

"What—?" Teresa protested.

"Teresa, hand me that phone," Duncan interrupted.

"Duncan," Teresa warned her husband, using the firm tone reserved for occasions when she wanted to have her way in no uncertain terms. "I have a right to know what's happening with my boys."

"It's police business," Duncan said.

Her disapproving sigh proceeded a click over the line, indicating she'd agreed but not happily so.

"Yes?" Duncan asked.

"Hector's out for blood. She's safe for now. We're at a hotel so Jules can rest. But when I caught up to her he already had her." Sean relayed what had happened at the truck stop, ending with, "He was planning to kill her. I didn't stick around for him to wake up and I'm not sure what happened. If they discover we were in there it won't look good—a dead body, Jules's prints, possible security cameras."

"You did the right thing," Duncan assured him.

"Hector saw me shift," Sean added. "There were no cameras in the room. I don't think he can prove it. He might have the impression I wore a mask."

Duncan didn't speak for a long moment. "He's a criminal. No one will believe him. You need to come home as soon as possible, Sean. We can take care of Jules here. It's time to circle the wagons."

"I don't know how wagons will help, but we'll be home tonight," Sean answered. He took a deep breath, not wanting to climb back into a small space with her and all the while knowing he had to. "She'll just have to sleep in the car. I should never have stopped."

JULES DIDN'T KNOW where she was going when she slipped out of the motel room. She just knew she needed to leave. Running had become second nature as if the sound of her feet hitting the pavement somehow erased whatever happened around her. She didn't make it five steps before a hand grabbed her elbow.

"Good, you're packed." Sean maneuvered her forcefully toward the truck. The strap on her shoulder slipped, causing her arm to drop under the weight. "We should get back on the road."

When he'd said he could track her, she had thought she'd make it more than three feet out of the door. Jules didn't protest. What was the point?

Sean locked her in the truck, grabbed the rest of their belongings from the motel room, checked out, and had them driving down the road within ten minutes. The vehicle bounced and Jules closed her eyes, exhaustion filling every limb. She let the numbness of sleep take over her. For the moment, she decided not to fight.

17

THOUGH THE HOUR was late when Sean pulled into Boston, Teresa had waited up for them, watching the passing cars from her front window. He saw her face as he drove by. The members of the Flaherty family lived within a three-block radius in their Southie neighborhood. Sean's home was two houses down from Duncan and Teresa, and across the street from Brian.

Sean lived in a square brick home technically owned by Fillan, who was helping him learn how to remodel whenever they had spare time, which wasn't often. The repairs had been slow going. It was more house than he needed as a single man, but it had come on the market after his arrival on Earth and since he'd saved Brian's life the family insisted Sean live close so they could protect him. With five bedrooms, Teresa said it was perfect for raising a family, and she often instructed him to bring a woman home. Carrying Jules's sleeping body up the front stairs to hide her from a sociopath was not how he imagined Teresa meant for that to happen.

Teresa appeared behind him carrying an armful of clothes, sheets and whatever else a woman might need. Sean wasn't exactly set up for the finer things. What little decoration he had around the room came from the Flaherty women taking pity on his bachelor ways.

"She looks thin," Teresa observed, her voice low to keep from waking Jules. The woman had a stern brown gaze. Her eyes pierced in a way only a mother's could, like she knew every secret and just waited for a confession. She saw everything, or at least gave the impression she did. Sean had a feeling she already knew all about Hector and Jules's trouble at the truck stop. Duncan never could keep things from his wife, just as marriage should be. "And worn. You should have let her rest at the motel."

"She's safer here in Boston than out on the road. You didn't need to bring sheets, I have—"

"Pish," she dismissed with a short chuckle. "I'll

bet you haven't even changed your bedding this week. It will take me only a moment."

He hadn't been home all week, but Sean didn't argue. Jules sighed in his arms but didn't open her eyes. He held her easily as Teresa changed the bedding. If he wanted to, he could have protested. It wasn't as if he lived dirtily. His home, though lacking in furnishings, was kept immaculate. However, Sean had learned never to dispute Teresa's good intentions. It was easier to let her have her way.

"You make sure you two come over in the morning for breakfast," she ordered on her way out the door. "Everyone will be there."

Sean laid Jules on the bed before going to lock his door. He kept an eye on Teresa through the front window as she walked back home. Even when she was no longer in sight, he was able to focus his shifter hearing on her footsteps. When she was safely inside, he said, "You could have said hello to her. She likes you."

He turned from the window to where Jules stood in the hallway. He knew when he'd laid her down she wasn't sleeping.

"And talk about what?" Jules joined him at the window. "Sorry about bringing yet another murderer to your family's door? Sorry about Brian almost being shot that one time, hope it doesn't happen again? No, thanks. I think I'll skip the awkward moment."

"Jules..." Sean let go of a long, wearied breath. He rubbed his forehead in frustration. "I'm too tired to deal with you right now. This new attitude of yours—"

"It's not new," she interrupted.

"It's new to me." Sean felt so many things when he looked at her—desire, rage, aggravation, hope. Torn between the desire to strangle her and the need to kiss her, he ran his hands through his hair, trying not to reach for her. "I don't understand you, Jules. You're so..."

Her expression hardened and a cold wall went up between them.

"What happened to you?" he asked. "Why is Hector after you?"

"You saved me from him today. You should know what you've gotten yourself into. I guess I owe you that much." Jules paced across his living room floor and paused long enough to kick off her shoes.

She traced a hand along the back of his blue couch and faced a large television he rarely had time to watch. The bookcase on one side was filled half with worn paperback mystery novels and half with DVD movies. It was how he learned about Earth culture and expanded his vocabulary. On the other side of the television, a black and white poster-size photo of a vase holding dried flowers hung on his wall, put there by Fillan's wife.

Jules didn't look at any one object for too long. "I saw Hector and Juanita shoot two prostitutes. One was just a kid, barely legal. I had the murders and other things on tape. I was going to drop it off anonymously to the police just as soon as I figured out who I could trust with it, but somehow Hector discovered I'd witnessed them."

"And how exactly were you there?" Tension rolled over him.

"I live in East Boston. Most of my neighbors are part of the Spanish speaking community. They're respectable people. Devout. Hard working. Honest. Giving. They feel sorry for me because I don't have family. I'm up to my eyeballs in *sangria* and *paella*."

Sean frowned. He stepped into her path to force her to either face him or turn around to continue her pacing.

She did neither, instead taking up residence by the window. "Like any community, a few rotten apples spoil the orchard. The Velázquez family is a blight. They terrorize, kill, traffic in drugs and immigrants. Everyone knows it, and no one knows how to stop them. We can't exactly wait around for someone to kill off the remaining two siblings. So, I decided to do something about it. I integrated myself into the club scene and watched them. Most of what I have is drug deals, a few assaults, but then I hit the mother lode."

"You hit a mother?"

"It means I found a lot of evidence." Jules swiped at her eyes. "I didn't think they'd kill them. I wanted to get them incriminating themselves on tape. I wanted them to say something concrete. Instead, they each pulled out a gun and shot those two girls. Juanita and Hector then argued. It got pretty heated. One of the girls had a family. Juanita laughed and said she would kill them all if they came sniffing around. Hector called her reckless. He said she should only use orphans in the trade so no one will look for them."

"Jules, what were you thinking?"

"That I could stop them," she answered defensively. "I did everything right. I took the tape and hid it in my apartment. I went about my life like usual so no one would notice anything. I told no one. I don't know how they found out I was there, but the next thing I know Hector's goons are chasing me from my gym and out of the city. I'd been on the run three days when I stole your car. I didn't know it was you. I saw a man with a fast car and thought you were an easy mark." She began to pace again. "I shouldn't even be here. They'll find me. They'll—"

"They'll find you with me. Let them come. I'm not frightened of them."

Lights steadily moved over the wall as a car passed outside. Jules automatically ducked back from the window, hiding against the wall. Her head turned to the side, her eyes fixed as she watched the taillights. "I should never have come back to Boston."

"They don't know my last name or where I live. They don't even know what I was driving. We're safe here for the night. You need to rest." Sean's mind raced. Though physically tired, he did not believe he could sleep. "I'll sit up."

She looked like she might argue. Glancing out of the window to find the street quiet, she finally nodded. "Make sure the doors are locked and your gun is loaded."

He couldn't help the small chuckle that escaped his lips. "Humans and their guns. I keep telling everyone I don't need the gun."

To his surprise, she smiled at him. "I've seen your dragon, and yet you look so...normal."

"I am normal."

"No. You're something extraordinary."

Jules's nearness called to him, and he lifted his hand to touch her. She whisked past, gracefully making her way down the hall to his room. He followed mindlessly, eyes glued to the lithe sway of her hips and the curve of her ass.

The lamplight in his bedroom illuminated Jules with a soft glow. He owned a king size bed because he liked to spread out when he slept. The plain black of his comforter contrasted the white sheets. As Jules crawled into the middle of it, he knew he'd gladly give up sleeping space to keep her there. She tilted her head as if commanding him to come to her.

"You have to admit..." He sat between her legs and lifted her foot to pull off her sock. He kissed the top of her toes before setting her foot back down. "We're good together." He took hold of her other foot and held it in his hands. "What if I told you I want you to stay here?"

"In Southie?" She waved her hand weakly to the side and wiggled her toes to get him to rub along the arch of her foot.

"With me. Here. In this house." He ran his thumb along her foot.

"You looking for a roommate?"

"A family," he corrected. "Don't you want a family?"

She didn't speak for a long moment as if contemplating that question. "In some ways, I feel like my eyes were shut most of my life. I grew up, I dated, I knew I would find a man and would have married and had babies as is expected. But then something happened, and that life was derailed. It left me wondering if I was simply sleepwalking through my existence. I'd accomplished nothing of worth. And in some ways that scares me more than being beaten near dead. I had nothing left. My mother had passed away. What I felt for you was a confused mess. I'd almost died in a dirty alley. I needed my life to mean more." She sighed heavily, running her fingers through her hair. "I don't know. I'm tired. I'm probably not making any sense."

Sean stared at the delicate strings of flesh that made the underside of her toes. He was aware of his eyes shifting as they focused on her skin, but he couldn't stop them. It had been a long time since he could shift without worrying someone might see who he was. A small scar curled around the side of the smallest digit with two smaller dots closer to the top. It almost looked like a mischievous smile and tiny crooked eyes. "There is nothing wrong with wanting an honorable life of meaning. That is why I came through the portal. I wanted my life to mean something to my people. I wanted to give them a future."

He felt the ticking of each second like some silent vortex pulling him into the fathoms of an infinite sea. The moment stretched, a measured instant that would decide between drowning and salvation. Sean forced his gaze to move from the grinning scar to her steady blue eyes.

Realizing she didn't answer his request she remained with him, Sean dropped her foot and stood. He did not understand these humans and their conflicted signals. "You should rest. I'll stay awake. We'll figure out how to deal with the Velázquez family in the morning."

18

A LOUD POP jolted Jules from a deep, dreamless sleep. Her heartbeat quickened, tinged with the panic and fear born of disorientation. A second, similar noise echoed from outside the room.

"Gun," she whispered as she scurried to roll off the bed. "Hector."

Sean instantly shifted to dragon form as his body reacted, ready for a fight. He tilted his head and pulled her back down with a taloned hand.

"Backfire," Sean corrected, changing back to his human form. "Car."

He slipped an arm around her waist, tugging gently to keep her on the bed. Now that immediate danger had passed, a fog clouded her mind, the world between dreams and life, the perfect haze that came from a long sleep. She felt a calmness that had eluded her for a long time. Jules stretched, her knuckles hitting against the hard wood of the headboard. She gave a contented sigh.

The mattress rocked as Sean's arm slid from her body. "I made you breakfast earlier, but it's cold now."

"Mmm, I don't care." She covered her mouth, suppressing a yawn. "I'm starved."

"I'll stick it in the microwave. Wait right here."

The bed moved again, and she watched as Sean left the room. She closed her eyes, the smell of him lingering over her senses, mingling with the fresh smell of soap and clean linens. Hearing a noise, she forced her eyes back open. She lazily watched as Sean carried a tray into the room. The smell of food woke her stomach, and it growled in response. She pushed up.

"I told Teresa we'd be over for a late lunch. I wanted to give you time to sleep." She watched the clean-shaven lines of his jaw as he talked. His wet hair was slicked back, still drying from a shower. He sat the flat tray down on the bed. The silver dish was more of a fancy serving platter than a breakfast tray. Jules didn't mind. Food was food, and the scrambled eggs, bacon and toast could have been served in a rusty frying pan, and she would still devour it at this point.

"Thank you." The words barely made it past her lips before she had the first forkful in.

Sean gave a small laugh. "Politeness? What happened to the surly tempered woman I've been traveling with?"

"I finally slept." She arched a brow. "So, you also cook?"

"All men on my planet cook. We don't have women to do it for us. No one was around to cook for my brother or me after our parents died. We had to learn or starve. It's a great motivator." An easy grin curled on his mouth as if he remembered something he wasn't sharing. The expression wasn't intentionally sexy, but it left her stomach fluttering and a very distinct tingle in her thighs. She chewed slowly, staring at his mouth as she ate. She took a moment to realize he stared back, not speaking.

"You have a brother?"

"Galen." His smile fell. "He probably thinks I'm dead. He asked me not to be the first to step through the portal, and I promised him I would see him again. When I did not return..."

"Maybe he'll come through, too?"

"Maybe. But the portals do not always appear in the same place. Earth is an immense planet. Even if he came, he would not find me. When I did not return, I imagine it caused a panic amongst the royals, and they might still be trying to decide if they should allow someone through again."

"It might not mean anything, but I heard a lizard man was living in the swamps of Louisiana." She didn't tell him it was gossip from Truckerman. "Maybe it was a sighting?"

"Perhaps." His tone did not sound hopeful.

"I'm sorry. I can't help feeling this is my fault. If I hadn't been out walking late at night, I would have..." Not knowing why she suddenly felt uncomfortable, she glanced at her plate. "I like the house."

"Mrs. Flanagan passed soon after my arrival and her son put it on the market. Brian said Mikey always claimed he was getting out of this neighborhood and never looking back, which I found odd because it's a perfectly fine human neighborhood. I would give anything to be able to see my childhood home again. My people don't move around from house to house to house like yours."

"Where did Mikey go?"

Sean laughed, a hypnotically beautiful sound. "Three blocks north."

Jules couldn't help herself. She chuckled as she bit into a piece of bacon.

"Fillan purchased it for me since I could not complete the transaction for obvious reasons, but I pay for it. The place was a disaster. Mrs. Flanagan smoked those cigarettes like a chimney every day for fifty years and had these two incontinent poodles she kept locked in a room during the day when she went to work. My first remodel project was to pull up the carpet and scrub every surface twice." Sean glanced around, pride shining in his eyes.

"You've done well for yourself, Sean." She nodded, swiping the crumbs from her fingers. They sprinkled the empty plate.

"Thank you." Sean took the tray and set it on the floor.

"And breakfast was wonderful."

"Thank you." When he again looked in her direction, his eyes narrowed carrying a predatory glint in their depths. The shifter thing should have scared her, but she wasn't afraid of him. She felt safer with Sean than with any other person.

"We should go."

"We have no place to be," he countered. "The Flahertys are looking for Hector. I told them we'd stay here. They want you to be safe."

"I don't need to be taken care of," she said. "I am not a victim."

"So you want to what? Continue to use yourself as bait in some misguided effort to regain control over your life? I can't change what happened, Jules. I wish I could, but I can't. Neither can you. We are where we are. What we can change is our future. You don't have to keep running."

"I'm not running. I'm doing something to make my world a better place." She stood and paced around the bedroom, staring at her bare feet. The shades were drawn, and the light dim. "When I was in the hospital, hurting like I've never hurt before, feeling sorry for myself, I heard some of the nurses talking. The girl on the other side of the curtain had been beaten, raped, shot. She slipped into a coma and then died after two weeks on life support. I followed that story as I recovered. It kept me strong because I knew that I'd gotten lucky, and that what happened to me could have been much worse."

"Jules." The nearness of his voice startled her, and she spun around to face his chest. "You're an amazing woman. So enduring." He touched her cheek, leaning in. His voice dropped. "So soft."

Sean flicked his tongue over the seam of her lips,

running it delicately along the inner ridge. With each pass, he probed deeper until his teeth nibbled and his mouth soothed. A primitive growl erupted from within, an animalistic sound filled with passion. His kiss deepened, consuming her thoughts in its adoring embrace.

Warm hands delved beneath her shirt, caressing her waist and back. When Sean touched her, she forgot herself. Apprehension melted away. He worked her clothing from her hips and legs before pulling her shirt over her head. Once he had her naked, he took his time re-exploring every inch of her body. His hand slid over her flesh, leisurely moving over her ass and thighs, the backs of her knees, her calves and ankles.

When he reached her feet, he kneeled on the floor. His face drew close to her sex as his piercing gaze looked up the length of her body. The dim light caressed the side of his face, contrasting his masculine features. Arousal surged, beginning between her thighs and making its way to her stomach and breasts.

Sean kissed her sex just as he had her mouth, slow at first and growing deeper with each pass. He cupped her breasts, massaging the nipples into hard, erect points. No man had ever made her body heat and her bones melt like this one did. Everything about him turned her world around.

Jules gasped, her head falling back as she closed her eyes. His tight grip on her hips kept her upright. He drank in her taste, nipping her with his teeth. Lips kissed and sucked in turn. He slid a finger inside her moist depths, rocking against the sweet spot buried there.

"Sean," she whispered.

He responded, but the words were lost in a raspy growl against her flesh. The finger inside her moved faster, taking her toward climax.

Outside, cars drove past, the slow, steady hum of their engines blending with the harsh pant of her breath. Sean moaned. She grabbed his head, jerking him up from the floor before she collapsed from pleasure. Pulling his shirt, she walked him to the bed. As soon as the backs of her legs touched, she sat. Sean threw off his shirt as she worked on his pants. Once she had him naked, she explored his lean hips, using their positions to run her fingers over his chest and arms.

The dim light sneaking past the curtains haloed his body. She kissed his stomach, feeling more than seeing the hard texture of his muscles. Jules moaned softly, drawing her lips along the thick shaft of his arousal. Her tongue dragged across his flesh as she licked him. Repeating her torment, she did it again and again. She twirled her tongue over the tip, liking the way his breath caught and held. His body tensed beneath her moving palms.

Sean lightly stroked her hair. Slowly, she sucked him between her lips, using her hands to cup his balls and stroke the extra length she couldn't fit comfortably into her mouth. His heady scent surrounded her as he moved his hips, following her direction.

She hadn't realized how much she'd missed him. They'd known each other so briefly, but that life-altering moment defined both of them. Sean felt like home, and she hadn't had that for a long time. His head fell back as he faced the ceiling. She sucked harder, took him deeper. He was close to release, and she wanted to give him that final, beautiful gratification.

Sean stopped her. With a forceful jerk, he pulled her off him and rolled her on the bed. Jules wanted to give him everything she had—her body, her soul, her heart. But was it fair to ask for his in return? Her life was complicated now, dangerous. She'd already taken him away from his family and friends. Hell, she'd taken him away from his entire planet. Now, he was on the Velázquez family's radar thanks to her. The last thing she wanted was to hurt him, but she kept putting him in danger. So, she swallowed her feelings deep and instead focused on the physical pleasure their bodies could make.

He fitted his legs between hers, parting her wide. His hands cupped her sex, stroking and pushing until she squirmed frantically for more. She vaguely heard her voice begging him to finish it.

Sean braced his weight, thrust inside her, going deep to maximize the pleasure. She practically screamed, enjoying the depth of his claim. With a sure hand, she reached between her thighs, stroking herself as he moved his hips. He kissed her breasts, biting gently.

Jules couldn't control her body as it tensed. Tremors racked her as she came and she climaxed hard. Sean only moved faster. When her body had given all it could, he let go, releasing himself inside her.

His weakened body collapsed over her, and he instantly pulled out and fell onto the bed to avoid crushing her with his weight. They lay next to each other, panting and hot, their bodies recovering from the mindless ecstasy. As reality set in, she rolled onto her side to face him.

"What's going to happen when this is all over?" She touched his chest, feeling more vulnerable than she liked.

"I don't know," he whispered, "I just don't know."

19

"MAN, Sean, you took long enough to find a girlfriend." Rory glanced out the window of his mother's kitchen to the backyard where Jules stood with Fillan's wife, Myrna. Like all the Flaherty men, Rory had distinct green eyes, thick brown hair, and a teasing expression. "I was beginning to wonder if all shifters lived like monks. Or maybe your little dragon wasn't standing at attention. You know, they have pills for that. Not sure what the pills will do to you, but—"

"My dragon is not little. It is unyielding, stands fine, and receives plenty of attention." Sean did his best not to look like he spied on Jules, even though that was exactly what he was doing. He was glad to see Jules smiled every once in awhile. Myrna had a generous nature though he'd seen her temper flare whenever she thought someone talked badly about her family. Her long, brown hair and equally dark eyes gave her an exotic beauty. Fillan was crazy about her. That's one thing Sean respected about the Flaherty clan. They knew the importance of family and loyalty. Cheating was still a concept Sean was trying to grasp. How one could betray a mate was beyond his comprehension, and he could only conclude that humans were genetically programmed differently.

"I think you are taking things too literal again. I meant your penis," Rory clarified.

"So did I." Sean grinned. He took Rory's playful words in stride, secretly thankful the man tried to lighten the mood. The Flahertys often dealt with stressful situations by using humor. As a family of cops, it's what kept them sane.

"Rory, you will not discuss penises in my kitchen," his mother scolded, hitting Rory's arm lightly.

"Sorry, Ma, I forgot." To Sean, Rory added, "Penises are clearly living room conversation."

"You leave Sean alone," Teresa ordered. "I don't

see you with a girl on your arm and a grandbaby in mine."

"That's because I can't find anyone who cooks as good as you, Ma," Rory said. Teresa swatted at him with her dishtowel, but the slight smile on her face revealed that she loved every charming thing her son said.

"No, you haven't found one that will put up with you," Sean said.

"Was that a barb?" Rory pretended to be shocked. "Well, done, alien. There may be hope for you yet."

"Rory," Teresa warned.

"Sorry, Ma," Rory mumbled.

Jules touched Myrna's arm briefly and started to back away, only to stiffen when Myrna grabbed her and gave her a hug. Jules's eyes met his. She arched a shocked brow, even as she patted Myrna in awkward affection.

The two women walked together toward the house. Suddenly, Jules stopped, glancing to the side. Sean couldn't see what she looked at from his position by the window, but he watched her expression fade for the briefest of seconds. She said something to Myrna, who nodded and headed toward the back door. Sean watched. Jules looked at him and gave a slight smile and a wave before walking out of view.

"Where's she going?" Sean asked, as soon as Myrna entered.

"Oh, she said she recognized someone she wanted to say hello to," Myrna answered. "She said to tell you she'd be back in a minute."

Sean frowned, not liking the fact Jules was out of his sight. Teresa beckoned Myrna to help carry food into the dining room where most of the men already sat and waited. As they left the room, Sean edged toward the back door, intent on bringing Jules inside.

"Sean!" Duncan yelled. "Come here. We have something."

Hearing the tone, he instantly changed course for the dining room. Duncan held a cellular phone to his ear, nodding as he wrote something down. The smell of roast beef, potatoes and corn on the cob filled the air. Only Rory touched the food, slowly picking at a dinner roll only to toss squished bits of it into his mouth. Energy coursed through Sean, making his limbs jittery as he waited for Duncan to hang up.

Seeing Sean's expression, Fillan said, "Hector's in town."

Duncan continued talking in hushed tones.

"What about your bond?" Rory asked. "You still have that drug dealer out."

"Actually, I checked," Brian inserted. "A patrol unit picked him up for driving under the influence. So he's back where he belongs."

"Good. That was my last one." Sean tried to answer and listen to Duncan at the same time. "But I have a few more coming up I could use help on."

"I'm game. I could use the extra cash," Rory said.

Duncan flipped his phone, shutting it. "That was Rohan. The truck stop reported vandalism, but nothing more. The crime scene guys are there now, and Columbia PD is on alert for the trucker's body. We'll let Maryland deal with it. We gave them the name of their killer." Duncan paused, leaning to glance into the kitchen. When he saw Jules wasn't there, he lowered his voice. "There's no reason to get Jules involved unless we have to. At most, she'll have to testify, but I hope it won't come to that. I'll keep you out of it. For now, let's take care of our problem here first."

Sean nodded in agreement. "Hector." A sick feeling knotted his stomach. Part of him felt like he should've just killed all of them when he had the chance while they lay helpless on the floor. The only problem was he wasn't a murderer. No matter how much they deserved it, he couldn't kill someone when they couldn't defend themselves. If it were in him, he'd have gone after the guys who beat up Jules years ago. They would never have made it to trial.

"Rohan's sitting on their house," Duncan said. "Hector showed up. He had two guys with him."

"What do we do? Sit and wait for them to make a move?" Rory asked. "Or do we try to draw them out?"

"I'm not using Jules as bait," Sean said.

"Where is Jules?" Duncan asked.

"She said she wanted to say hi to someone outside," Myrna answered.

"Who?" Duncan demanded.

"I don't know. I saw no one." Myrna frowned. "Why? What's wrong?"

"You don't think she'd run off, do you?" Teresa inquired. "Once a person starts running, it's some-times hard for them to stop."

"Damn it," Sean swore. Yes, actually, he did think that. He ran out of the front door to search the sidewalk. He took a deep breath, trying to catch her scent, and narrowed his eyes to focus on the distance. Jules was nowhere to be found.

"Shit, Sean, watch your face," Rory said, moving to block him from the view of the street. "You can't do that out here."

Sean didn't care if he was exposed. He needed to find her. Now.

20

—

Jules slipped the cab driver a couple of bills and stepped out of the car. All she had on her were the clothes Myrna loaned her and the wad of cash she'd stolen from Sean in her pocket. It had been a long ride from Southie to the isolated area of East Boston and regret filled her even as she knew she couldn't remain with Sean. If she stayed, she'd only put them in danger. It wasn't fair to him. He had built a life in Southie, and it was clear the Flahertys had made him part of their family. She cared for him enough to leave him. If and when she finished this, she could consider a future.

Though several new restaurants and condominiums were going up along the harbor, rent had increased more slowly in East Boston than in other parts of the city. It was what she could afford on wait-ressing wages. Her apartment was a block away from where the cab pulled over, but she wanted to sneak in without being seen. The tenants all knew the secret way in.

Jules ventured down a side alley and began the long trek up the fire escape of the building next to hers. Once to the top, she climbed over the side, crossed the roof and then paused. She looked over the edge, feeling her stomach lurch a little at the long drop. It wasn't a far leap to the top of her building, and she'd done it once before, but the danger of the fall caused her legs to shake.

Jules took a deep breath and pushed off. Her body flailed a little as she flung through the air. With a hard thud, she landed on the other side, stumbling forward on the loose gravel.

A woman with a cigarette met her eyes from the far corner. She sat, hidden by the landscape along the roof's ledge. Jules recognized her as a fellow tenant, though she had little contact with her in the past. Not saying a word, the woman watched her while taking a long drag off her cigarette. Smoke curled over the woman's head, dissipating quickly as it caught in the chilled breeze.

"Hey," Jules said, by way of greeting, angling her jaw slightly. "How's it going?"

The woman answered by taking another puff. Dark, intense eyes ringed with heavy black makeup stared in hostile boredom.

Normally a person would have to fit through a narrow window with a broken latch to sneak inside, but the smoker had placed a brick in front of the roof access door, and Jules was able to get in unhampered. Hurrying down the narrow stairwell, she stopped to listen for people on the other side of the door before entering the top-level hallway. The faint trace of *corrido* music radiated into the hall from one of the apartments, warring with the steady thump of hip-hop from another. Since most people took the elevator, she went to the stairs.

She'd lived in the building for several years, and duly recognized it as home, yet Jules still felt removed from her surroundings. The familiar yellowed walls and the slightly moldy smell of the stairwell no longer permeated with safety. She'd been hiding here, away from life, away from Sean and anyone else who mattered from her past. Though she made new friends, found a new life, it wasn't a full one and the people she met were never close. Jules had successfully managed to keep them at arm's length, putting a wall up so they never really got to know her.

She thought of Sean. There was something incomplete about his life, though not nearly as drastic as hers. Jules had fought so hard to demonstrate she was strong that she had stunted herself in a whole new way. Her emotions had been blocked, and her obsessive vigilante mission to prove she wasn't a victim had taken over her life, creating an overwhelming contradiction, as she became a victim yet again.

Coming out of the stairwell on her floor, she hurried down the hall toward her apartment. Part of her expected to see the door off the hinges and the place trashed. The door was intact. She hesitated when she realized she didn't have a key to the place. Knowing there was no way around being seen by at least one person, she went to her neighbor's and knocked. The hardwood creaked, and a young girl stuck her head into the small opening. Wide, brown eyes looked up at her from a pretty face.

"*Como estas, gata?*" Jules leaned down, smiling. She kept her voice quiet.

The four-year-old grinned as Jules called her a cat. "*Miau,*" she meowed like a kitten by way of answer. When her brothers and sisters went to school, little Adelina had no one to play with during the day. She'd taken to pretending to be a cat since they weren't supposed to have pets in the apartments. "Is mama home?"

"*Miau*," she answered, nodding.

"Is she sleeping?"

"*Miau*." Again a nod.

"Let's not wake her, *gata*." Jules glanced up and down the hall, making sure no one saw her speaking to the child. "Do you remember those keys I gave to mama?"

The child nodded.

"Do you know where she put them?"

Adelina shrugged, tilted her head to the side and thought about it, then nodded excitedly. She took off into the apartment before Jules could ask her to get them. Jules heard rummaging and a loud crash. She grimaced, and pushed the door to the apartment to make sure Adelina was all right.

The child stood on a stool, her arms reached to the side, her mouth opened wide in surprise. Pieces of porcelain, remnants of a white pot and its contents, lay scattered on the floor—coins, paperclips, a small pocketknife, and cigarette lighter.

"Ade...?" A sleepy, panicked Dania ran into the room to check on her daughter. The woman worked nights while her husband was home with the kids. Her only time to rest was while the oldest were in school. Despite the busy schedule, her house was tidy. Seeing her daughter on the stool, she tiptoed through the porcelain shards to get the child down, all the while speaking in low, scolding words of concern.

"I'm sorry, Dania, I asked her if she knew where my spare key was," Jules said.

Dania jolted in alarm as she turned with her daughter on her hip. The two were definitely mother and daughter with the same round eyes and softly curled hair. Her softly accented voice might have sounded breathy, but Jules knew the woman had a set of lungs on her when called for. "Jules? Where have you been? How are you?"

"It's a long story. I stopped by for my key." Jules leaned over and began picking up shards, placing them into her hand.

Dania carried her daughter to the couch and set her down, telling her to sit and not move as punishment for opening the door without permission. Adelina pouted her lower lip and growled the cutest sound. She sounded like an angry feline. She crossed her arms and refused to look at her mother as she stared at a wall.

"I don't have your key," Dania said, coming to help Jules pick up. She piled shards on her palm. "Your brother was here. He wanted to know if I was the neighbor who had your key and asked to be let in."

"Brother?" Jules frowned.

"He's not like I would have pictured," Dania continued. "But, then, that might be why you never speak of him." Suddenly, her expression fell. "It was all right that I gave him the key, wasn't it? He said you had emergency gallbladder surgery and sent him to my door. He knew my name, your work schedule... He was supposed to get me the hospital room information so I could stop by, but..."

"I don't have a brother," Jules said, all the pieces she'd picked up slipping off her hand back onto the floor. "When did he come?"

"A few days ago. I saw him leave with a bag in his hands. I thought he was bringing you a change of clothes."

Jules didn't know whether to cry or scream.

"He knew everything about you, Jules," Dania insisted. "I didn't just give it to a stranger. He knew... *No entiendo.* I don't understand what is going on."

Jules didn't hear the woman's words. Her heart pounded hard and heavy in her chest, nearly choking her. She crossed to a small window on the far side of the room and opened it, taking a deep breath of air.

"*Lo siento*," Dania said. "I'm sorry, Jules."

"It's all right," Jules assured her, even though she didn't feel it. Dania was a friend, though they weren't close. She'd kept her distance, even when Dania tried to connect.

Jules crawled out of the window onto the ledge. She looked down, wobbling nervously at the height.

"Jules? What are you doing?" Dania demanded, trying to grab hold of her arm.

"I'll be fine," Jules assured her. A tight feeling cinched her gut as she saw the alleyway several stories below. For a moment, she wondered what it would be like to fall, the air hitting her face, twisting her hair. She took another step, edging toward her apartment as she hugged her back along the side of the building. Jules wasn't the kind of woman to jump.

She carefully bent over and peeked inside her home. Nothing immediately appeared out of the ordinary. The hard stone bit into her hand as she held the precarious position, watching and listening. Maybe whoever broke into her place didn't find what they were looking for.

"Jules?" Dania asked, leaning out of her apartment window. "Is everything all right?"

Jules nodded, moving to slap her palm against the window frame. The vibrations in the wood made the catch jiggle until it loosened and swung open just as she knew it would. She pushed up, letting herself inside. The window wouldn't stay up without help and once it lowered the air surrounding her became stale.

A tremor worked over her body. She looked over the living room. A small television sat on the coffee table she'd shoved against the wall. Before bed, she always put the remote to the right of the unit. It now sat on her quilt-covered couch. Next to it, she saw the faintest outline, a recess in the quilt. The indentation could be that of a person's backside? Could it belong to Jules's mystery brother? The idea of Hector or one of his goons in her apartment desecrated her sanctuary and the home no longer felt safe.

As soon as she retrieved the recording, she intended on packing what she could and getting out of there. Jules grabbed a bat from against the wall for protection and stealthily made her way through the house. Confirming she was alone, she set the bat aside and went to her bathroom.

The great thing about modern technology was

that everything had become much more compact. Instead of a giant VHS tape that required a monstrously sized camcorder like when she was a kid, the slim look of her recorder with a built-in memory card fit into her palm and hid with ease.

She kept the lights off and crawled onto her sink basin. Hanging from the ceiling on a chain, the light fixture swung back and forth when she bumped it. A decorative metal plate covered the base, and all she had to do was turn the screw a couple of times to get it to slide over the side. The metal plate covered not only the wiring but also a much larger hole in the plaster. Reaching inside, she felt the cool texture of a plastic bag and pulled the handheld out. Jules replaced the plate and hopped down.

"All this trouble over a little thing like you," she mused, studying it to make sure the unit was still intact. Then, remembering the death it showed, she sobered.

Jules hated to think of what she'd witnessed. The scenario had played itself in her head several times since it happened. For the most part, she could compartmentalize her feelings and push the details away. But now, as she held the recorder, she remembered the women's whimpers, felt their fear as she forced herself to stay and watch.

Why hadn't she tried to stop it? Jules should have known they'd shoot the girls. She replayed it over and over in her mind. Did she miss a detail? A look? A signal? All she wanted was to catch the two siblings confessing their human trafficking and other numerous crimes on tape. Instead, she'd recorded a murder.

"Don't worry, girls. I won't let you down again."

"Do you see anything?" Sean craned his neck to look around the East Boston neighborhood. This wasn't his part of town, and he only vaguely recognized a few of the landmarks. "I should get out of the car. You go home to your family. I can take care of things from this point."

Brian learned Jules's address from the police station. Rohan watched the Velázquez house. Teresa and Myrna waited at home. Rory, Fillan, and Duncan were checking out places in Southie—gas stations, taxis, the main roads. So far there was no sign of her.

"I'm not leaving you. Stop trying to send me home." Brian turned the car and slowed, glancing from the road to the passing buildings. With the busy streets packed with cars, it would be a few minutes before they found parking, even with the siren sitting on the dash of his unmarked black sedan. Under his breath, he added, "We're all tired of seeing you unhappy."

Sean frowned. "What are you talking about? We who?"

"Your family," Brian answered.

"Galen...?" Sean frowned.

"I mean us, Sean. We are your family. Can't you see that? You are like a brother to me. I'm not leaving you to deal with this on your own, just as you wouldn't leave me if I needed help. Jules matters to you, so she matters to us."

"Yes. You are my family, and Jules is my life." Sean looked out the window, unable to believe he'd admitted it out loud. "I can't lose her again. I should have found her last time, but this planet is so...different. I know more now. I can be more to her now."

"Does she feel the same way?"

"I don't...want to talk about it." Seeing the address they were looking for, he reached for the door handle before the car even stopped. "There it is."

"Sean, wait." Brian pulled Sean's jacket to keep him from jumping out. "Let me park the car."

"You park. I'm finding Jules." Sean hopped out as Brian hit the brakes. He landed with a slight stumble but didn't stop as he made his way to the front of the building. Grabbing his wallet, he pulled out a lock pick and opened the front door in a few smooth movements. The weighted front door hardly provided protection, especially when paired with a broken security camera hanging in the front lobby. The cracked lens would distort any image even with the camera turned on.

Sean went straight to the elevators. He knew she'd be here. It's where he'd be if he had evidence hidden of two murders. Jules thought she could protect him by running away. Didn't she realize he'd always come after her?

Sean impatiently tapped the elevator button as if doing so would make the machinery move faster. Maybe she didn't know he'd come. His behavior was not consistent in that regard. He hadn't gone after her two years ago. He'd just let her run. That was one mistake he would not be making again. This time, he'd fight for what was his.

2 2

JULES TOOK the stairs two at a time, making her way back to the rooftop. She still didn't know how Hector discovered she witnessed the murders. She had seen no one watching her that night, but apparently someone had. There was no telling who looked for her, and she wouldn't risk walking out the front door. The Velázquez family had people everywhere—from the dealers on the street corners to runners to those who owed them money. Any number of them would be desperate or greedy enough to turn her in for a small fee.

The smoker was gone from her corner, leaving behind a large scattering of cigarette butts. Jules hurried to the edge of the building, pushing up on one foot to balance on the side. The cold wind hit her face. The temperature had dropped since she'd arrived. She'd changed her clothes, wearing jeans, t-shirt, and a light black jacket. She looked across, ready to leap when a figure caught her attention. Stewie stood on the opposite rooftop with that irritatingly leering smile of his.

Jules pushed back, turning even before her feet completely left the edge. Jose stood behind her. She screamed, flailing her arms to stop her descent toward the rooftop and into the goon's arms, but she couldn't fight gravity. Jose grabbed her, gripping her tight as he forcibly swung her around. She heard Stewie land behind them, cursing as his feet skidded. The unmistakable click of a cocking gun sounded over them.

"Are you finished with me?" The smoker stood near the doorway, wearing a wounded look on her face as she rubbed her upper arm.

"Get out of here," Stewie ordered.

"What about my boyfriend's debt?" the woman insisted.

"Tell him he's got two months to come up with the cash," Jose conceded, as he dragged Jules with him to the door. The woman ran ahead of them, the sound of her footfall hitting heavy on the stairwell before the door slammed shut.

"What? Your boss not man enough to come himself?" Jules struggled, kicking her heel back at Jose's leg. Yelling up here would do no good. No one would hear her where they were.

"He doesn't waste his time with the trash," Stewie said. Jose's grip tightened.

"So, what? That makes you his garbage man?" Jules asked. "You should try working for the city. At least you can respect those guys."

"I have respect—" Stewie yelled, pointing a gun at her head. The hammer was pinned back, and all it needed to go off was the slight pull of the trigger. "Want me to show you—"

"She's just trying to rile you," Jose interrupted, only to growl in Jules's ear, "Shut up, or I'll shut you up. If you fall off the building, no one will think anything of it."

"Try it, asshole." Jules jerked against him. "I can just imagine how much your boss will like you coming back empty-handed."

"Hector's got some junk in the car. A quick shot of the good stuff will shut her up." Stewie pulled the door open.

"I'll scream the whole way down," Jules said.

"We'll burn down this building with everyone in it," Stewie warned. By the look in his eyes, she knew he would, and he'd probably enjoy doing it. The grotesque mixture of pleasure and anticipation made her skin crawl.

Jules didn't know what she should do next. She wanted to fight. She needed this to be over. Jose continued to haul her down the steps, but Jules was not going to make it easy for him. She dragged her feet and kept her body stiff. "Someone will see us."

Jose threw her down the last five steps. Tripping, Jules's body slammed hard into the wall. He grabbed her before she could right herself.

Stewie lifted his gun. "Shut up and walk."

They led her down the empty hall of the top floor. Earlier, there had been music from a few of the apartments. Now, it was silent. Stewie went ahead to the elevator and pushed the button. Jules watched the double doors intently, hoping to see help revealed on the other side. Jose loosened his grip, but the hard press of a gun barrel to her back instantly replaced it. The elevators dinged. Jules tensed. The shiny metal doors slid apart, seeming to take an abnormally long time to disclose the inside box was empty.

"Alert anyone and we'll shoot them." Jose pushed her into the elevator.

Jules didn't know what she should do. If she yelled for help on the street and these men opened fire on a crowd of innocent people, she'd never forgive herself. The problem with men like this is that they felt they could do anything without consequence. She chose to fight, to not be a victim, to be in that alley with a camcorder. The people on the street did not.

Feeling the press of metal deepen into her back, she glanced up. The elevator hit the ground floor and opened. A couple of people stood by the wall of mailboxes, flipping through envelopes. Outside, the traffic was heavy on the streets. A crowd walked by, not paying any attention to the trio coming to the front door. Jules kept her mouth shut and waited for her chance to escape.

23

SEAN CURSED as he hurried through every room of Jules's apartment. The modest place had a comfortable feel to it, but he couldn't picture her there. No, the only place he could envision Jules was in his home. He refused to imagine her anywhere else.

Each room he searched added to the terrible ache in his chest. She wasn't there. Stopping in her bedroom, he took a deep breath. The scent of her lingered and the clothes she'd borrowed from Myrna lay in a crumpled pile on her floor.

Feeling helpless, he hurried through the house. How long ago had she been there? Where would she go? To the police? Back to his home? Or would she run again?

"Jules," he whispered, rushing to the door. He

had to get to Brian. Together, they could search the whole building. As he hurried to the elevator, he pulled out his cellular and dialed. When he held it to his ear, he didn't get a signal. Sean forcibly hit the button and glanced up. The elevator was going down, and it would be several moments before it came back depending on its stops. Unable to force himself to wait, he entered the stairwell and began the long journey down. Sensing he was alone in the stairwell, he risked shifting and jumped over the railings, falling down a level at a time. The natural armor covering his legs and ankles absorbed the hard landings.

As he reached the bottom floor, he hid his dragon from view. A light sheen of sweat beaded his brow. A couple near the mailboxes looked at him curiously, but Jules was nowhere to be seen. He kept going, scanning his surroundings as he rushed outside.

Cold air hit his face, and he took a deep breath. Redialing Brian's number, he hurried down the sidewalk looking for Jules. Small clusters of people blocked his path, creating dense sections between open spaces. He held the phone to his ear, listening as it rang.

"Yeah?" Brian asked.

"She's not there, but she was. Where are you?"

Sean hurried past the pedestrians, barely giving them a second look. "I—"

Sean stopped walking. Across the street, he caught a glimpse of her. Jules's blonde streaked hair blew around her face as Stewie pushed her down into the backseat of a dark blue sedan. Next to him, Hector gave orders. Jose stood on the far side of the car.

"Sean?" Brian demanded through the phone.

"They have her," he whispered, compelled to act. He shut his phone, running into traffic. He pushed against the hood of a car and propelled his body forward. Horns honked and tires screeched. Reaching the other side, he yelled, "Jules!"

At the sound of her name, she shoved away from the open car to find him. Stewie turned, revealing the handgun he had trained on her. Jules's wide fear-filled eyes met his. Her lips parted as if she would speak. Stewie didn't hesitate. Sean responded, acting on instinct. He automatically began to shift. This is not where he wanted a fight to go down, but he had to protect her. Everything he was depended on it.

Hector took a few seconds longer, but he drew a gun. Sean lifted his fist, feeling the talons extending from his fingertips. Teeth elongated in his mouth.

"What the fuck?" Stewie charged forward and fired.

Screams erupted, the fervent sound of panic all around. Adrenaline coursed through Sean's veins, pumped by a heart that hammered violently. He felt the bullet whiz past but didn't stop. Stewie took a second to re-aim and fired. Sean leaped forward and slammed his palm into the center of the man's chest. Stewie flew back, crashing into the car. Another bullet soared, this time from Hector's weapon and Sean vaguely heard it strike metal behind him.

"I'm not scared by your parlor tricks." Hector popped off several more rounds.

Sean weaved, but he couldn't dodge them all. Fire burned his arm as a bullet found its target. It didn't matter. He had to get to Jules. Jules screamed, bringing her hand down on Hector's arm to throw him off balance.

As Hector turned his weapon toward Jules, Sean reacted. He darted forward, shifting completely as he reached for the man's throat. In seconds, it was over. Hector gurgled and slumped against the car.

Jules looked as if she might run to him, but her waist was pulled back into the car, keeping her halfway in and halfway out of the vehicle to serve as a human shield to the backseat. Someone had a hold of her. A gun appeared over her shoulder seconds before Jose peered out at him. Sean couldn't stop. He couldn't lose Jules. Not again. He couldn't let anyone hurt her.

"What the fuck is that thing?" Jose demanded. "Get in the car, bitch."

Sean yelled, letting all the frustration and panic he felt into the tortured sound. Jules flung her body, slamming into Jose's arm. The gun fired close to her head, the bullet flying toward the sky. Jose dropped the weapon. Sean tried desperately to find an opening to strike, but with the way Jules jerked around in Jose's embrace, he couldn't risk hitting her.

To his relief, Sean saw Brian wielding his police issued handgun, creeping around the opposite side of the car. The backseat doors were both open, and Brian aimed inside, ordering, "Drop it now and let her go!"

"What the fuck is that thing?" Jose demanded in panic, more worried about Sean than Brian's gun. Brian grabbed Jose from behind. Jules fell forward to her hands and knees.

Sean shifted back to his human form and reached to pull Jules into his arms.

"What thing?" Brian asked, pretending like he had seen nothing.

"But, but..." Jose mumbled in Spanish, clearly shaken up.

"You're hallucinating. What did you take? It will be easier for you if you tell us what you're on," Brian answered.

Jules held onto Sean. An eerie silence surrounded them, punctured only by the soft hum of abandoned car motors. Drivers and passersby had run for cover when the shooting started.

"Sean," Jules croaked. Now that the danger had passed, and she was safe, he let himself draw a calming breath. Brian had Jose against the car.

"Stay back," Sean ordered. He let go of her to check Hector and Stewie for a pulse. Brian handcuffed Jose. As soon as they had the scene secured, Sean pulled Jules to him once more. It felt so right to hold her. He planned never to let go. Quietly, he whispered, "Damn it, Jules. Why didn't you wait for me?"

"I didn't want anyone to get hurt." Jules trembled, feeling so delicate in his arms. "This is my mess."

"When will you learn? I'm not letting you go. Your mess is my mess. I care for you. I love you. I have from that very first night here on Earth." Fear of what might have happened still gripped him, but that's not the only reason he confessed his feelings for her. They were as true now as at any other moment. "I will never stop loving you. The only thing that can truly hurt me is not being able to protect you."

"Sean." Dark blue eyes met his, piercing into him with the intensity of her emotions. "I—"

Police sirens echoed around them, but with traffic at a standstill, they couldn't get too close.

"Don't say a thing when the police get here," Brian ordered. "I'll take care of everything."

Jules moved awkwardly against Sean and yet he wouldn't let go. She reached into the front of her jacket to pull out a small camcorder. "Brian, you're going to need this. It's everything I have on Hector and Juanita. You're the only people I know to trust with it."

Brian took the device and slid it into his inside pocket. Uniformed police officers surrounded them, weapons were drawn as they tried to determine the situation. Jules was yanked from Sean's arms as a cop moved to handcuff him. He wasn't worried about being arrested, not with Brian flashing his badge. As an officer led Jules away from the scene, she glanced back at him.

"I love you, too," she yelled, not seeming to care

that everyone heard her. Brian's eyes met his, and he gave a small, quick smirk before turning back to the other police to explain what was happening.

Sean grinned, even as the officer pushed the cuffs a little too tightly into his wrists. Jules loved him. Nothing else mattered.

JULES WASN'T sure how she'd feel walking into a courtroom to face Juanita, but she knew when the time came, she would. It took hours for the police to sort through the chaos of her life. By the time the district attorney showed up at the station to talk to her, Jules had found an inner calm. One look at the attorney's salivating expression as he watched the murder tape and Jules knew she was in a position of power.

"Let me make this simple," she said before the man could even get started with his plans for her. They sat in one of the interrogation rooms. It was just like she'd seen in movies—a long mirror on one wall next to a door, and an old collapsible table with uncomfortable chairs. "I'll testify about everything you see on that tape and more, but only if no harm comes to Sean Flaherty over today's shooting. He saved my life."

"I'm not sure I can—" the attorney began, swiping at his balding head.

"You can," Jules assured him. "Because you need me to verify how that recording was made, and that it is real, and my testimony can bring down a crime family."

"Let me make a call." The man left the room. Jules looked at her clasped hands, trying to be patient as she waited for him to come back. She knew she wasn't under arrest, but understood that it would be better for her, and for Sean if she didn't get up and leave. When the door opened again, it was Brian.

"What's happening with Sean?" she demanded, stiffening with worry. "Is he all right?"

"Funny, he keeps asking me the same thing about you. He sent me to check on you," Brian said. "How are you holding up?"

"They're not arresting him, are they? You told them that he shot in self-defense. Stewie fired first," Jules said, before adding loudly toward the two-way mirror for the benefit of anyone listening. "He rescued me. He's a hero."

"No one is there," Brian said. "And I told them.

So did about fifteen witnesses."

"Do they know about," she finished her sentence by mouthing, "the dragon?"

"No. I think we're good there. Everyone was running for cover," Brian assured her. "And so far no one is asking too many questions about who he is."

"Then what's taking so long?"

"They're just trying to sort out this whole ordeal," Brian said. "They have two dead bodies and a gunfight in the middle of East Boston to account for. The Feds aren't too pleased that Hector Velázquez is dead. And then there is the matter of your credibility."

"My credibility is fine. I've never been convicted of anything," Jules dismissed.

"There's a lot of crime discussed on that recording."

"You're welcome," Jules answered, knowing he wasn't exactly thanking her with that observation.

"They're going to want answers as to how and why you have it," Brian insisted.

"And they'll get them. They'll offer me immunity for anything they think I might have done, and I'll take it, and they'll get their testimony. We both know any petty shit they think I did won't add up to taking down Juanita Velázquez and her crew."

"Damn, Jules. I don't know if I'm more impressed by, or frightened of, your cunning right now."

"I want to see Sean." Jules knew the sinking feeling wouldn't leave her until she saw him. When he said he loved her, she'd felt something she hadn't for a long time—hope.

"You will. Soon." Brian sat down at the table across from her. "They know Stewie's reputation. Jose isn't talking, but Myers is in there with him. He might be a lawyer, but the man can do his job. That prosecutor will have Jose begging for a deal by the time he's done with him. With Jose's testimony, your evidence, and the case files we already have on the Velázquez family, Juanita will be going away for a long time. Before now, they haven't had enough hard evidence to put her behind bars. You've done a good thing, Jules. You helped a lot of people who couldn't help themselves."

The district attorney came back into the room. "You have yourself a deal, Ms. Dalton. We will not be pressing charges against Mr. Flaherty."

"Good. Can I go now?" She made a move toward the door.

"It's best if you wait here. Someone is going to come talk to you about temporary police protection until we can find a more permanent solution," Myers said. "Things are going to be very dangerous and chaotic for while after we arrest Juanita. Hector being dead works in your favor. He can't come after you. But the Velázquez family has connections."

"I don't want protection," Jules stated.

"I don't think you comprehend the severity of this Ms. Dalton," Myers said. "It is my understanding that you live alone in East Boston."

"I recorded the video. Believe me, I understand how severe this situation is," Jules answered. "I won't be staying in East Boston. I have some place I can go. Brian will know how to contact me."

"She'll be safe," Brian assured the man when Myers glanced at him for confirmation.

The attorney looked as if he might protest, but in the end nodded in agreement. "Fine, but I want you to check in regularly. We'll be talking to you soon."

"Yes," Jules said.

When they were again alone, Brian chuckled. "I don't think he wanted to argue with you." He stood, motioning for Jules to join him. "I can't believe I've ever seen him speechless before."

"Smart man," Jules answered, too tired to back the words up with a smile.

"Where will you stay?" Brian asked, holding the door open for her.

"What better place to hide out than with a family of cops?" This time, she managed a smile. "That is if Sean wouldn't mind a roommate."

Brian chuckled and slipped his arm over her shoulders. "You know, I have a feeling he'll insist upon it."

"Rohan, it's me, where is Juanita?" Sean asked into his cellular, stepping out of the police station. They'd been detained for hours and evening now set over the sky.

"*Fuego*," Rohan answered. "Fillan is inside the club keeping an eye on things."

"Her brother just died, and she's at a bar? Now that's love," he noted sarcastically. Sean lifted his arm, hailing a cab. "Hold tight. I'll be there soon."

"What about Jules?"

"I sent her home with Brian. I want her safe-guarded." Sean knew he didn't have to say more. Rohan would understand, as would the rest of the family. "This is the only way to guarantee her wellbeing."

Sean would not fail to protect her. He didn't care what happened to him as long as Jules was safe.

25

Jules hugged her arms around her waist, staring out the window of the cab as it pulled up to *Fuego*. She couldn't believe that Sean thought she'd just go to his home and wait for him to finish rescuing her from her life choices. He hadn't even stopped to say goodbye.

After overhearing him with Brian at the station, she knew what she had to do. Ditching Brian hadn't been hard. She'd simply asked him to go back inside the station to get the purse she'd "accidentally" left behind. Gentleman that he was he agreed and Jules hailed the first cab that came her way.

Fuego lived up to its name, "Fire". She didn't have to go inside to know the stylistic metal sculptures created the illusion of giant flames as red and

215

orange lights flashed over them. The gently flickering colors could be seen beneath the bottom edge of the door. Loud music pumped throughout the club every night but Sunday. Jules didn't mind the job most days. Sure, she hated her bosses and the crimes, but the waitressing itself wasn't bad.

Walking past a group of women, Jules pulled a scarf from a purse. Without breaking stride, she wrapped it around her head to cover her hair. Pulling a bill out of her pocket to pay the cover charge, she had every intention of walking through the front door.

"What the hell are you doing here?" Sean growled, jerking her around, so she faced his chest. Jules gasped. "You're supposed to be with Brian."

"What the hell do *you* think *you're* doing here?" She mimicked his tone.

"Protecting you." Sean tugged her arm. "Come on. I'm putting you into a cab. Fillan will escort you home."

Jules resisted. She opened her mouth to protest.

Suddenly, the *pop-pop-pop* of gunfire sounded from inside the club followed by multiple shouts. Screaming patrons ran through the front doors, shoving the bouncer out of the way as they tried to escape what was happening inside. Sean swung Jules up over his shoulder and rushed her away from the mob. She kicked her feet, half in protest, half in an effort not to fall. Sean flung her off his shoulder and pressed her against a brick wall as he covered her with his body. His back blocked her face and kept her from seeing what was happening.

"Sean, stop, let me..." She tried to wiggle free.

He spread his arms to the side, using his body as a shield.

"Sean..."

"By all the gods, Jules, let me— " Sean's phone rang, interrupting him.

The sound of running feet and screeching car tires took the mob away, and was replaced by authoritative police shouts and sirens. She stopped her struggle to listen. He didn't move away from where he had her pressed to the wall. He grabbed his phone and flipped it open with one hand. "Yeah?"

Jules tried to listen to the other side of the conversation, but couldn't hear over the ambulance sirens moving up the street.

"I understand." Sean hung up. He gave one last look around the area before stepping away to let her free. "The FBI picked up Juanita behind the club."

"Thank goodness." Jules sighed.

Sean frowned. "What are you doing here?"

"Why are you surprised that I came? You think I like the idea of you coming out here to do some sort of vigilante justice?"

"Is that what you thought? We're here to arrest her. Well, Fillan is. I'm just here to make sure she doesn't get away. I want to know firsthand that Juanita is off the streets."

Relief filled Jules. "I thought you were going to kill her."

Sean shook his head in denial. Before he could answer, Juanita appeared with an escort of five FBI agents. Her hands were cuffed behind her back. Two men held her upright as they forced her to walk down the uneven alleyway in her stiletto heels.

"Only if forced." Sean's gaze trained on the crime boss.

Cold, defiant eyes found Jules. Suddenly, Juanita smiled, a truly threatening look that caused Jules to take hold of Sean's arm.

They watched as Juanita was shoved into the back of a police car. As the vehicle took the woman away, Sean led Jules toward the curb and lifted his arm to gesture at Fillan standing near the bouncer. "You shouldn't have come here. I wanted you to be safe."

"John," Fillan yelled. "Take care of them!"

A uniformed officer glanced at Sean and Jules before giving Fillan a thumbs-up. John approached. "Hey, Sean. You two need a lift back?"

"Yes, thank you." Sean threaded his arm over Jules's shoulders and followed the officer. They climbed into the back of John's squad car.

"What makes you think it will end with Juanita's arrest?" Jules slid her body close to Sean, keeping her voice low as John drove them home. She rested her hand on his leg, liking the way his automatically covered hers.

"Hector's dead. I didn't plan it like that, but it happened," Sean said.

"Juanita is the last of the Velázquez family," John inserted from the front seat. "Unfortunately for her, she's not very well liked. Half of what the authorities have on her is from her own men. I don't think they exactly liked taking orders from a woman."

"They couldn't arrest her because they didn't have outside collaboration," Sean added. "You gave them that."

"So it's over," she said in awe.

"Almost," Sean corrected. "You still have to testify. I don't think there is any way around it. They need you to give context to the recording."

Jules saw John's eyes on them through the

rearview mirror and didn't answer. She wasn't in a trusting mood and had a feeling it would be some time before she looked at strangers with anything but suspicion. Sean placed his arm over her shoulders, joining her in silence for the long ride home. When they reached Southie, Sean thanked the officer and ushered her inside.

"Brian tells me you plan on staying here," he said, shutting the door. His tone was light yet strained as if forced to be playful. He locked the door.

Jules smiled, even as some of her insecurities churned inside her. "You did say you love me or was that just the heat of the moment?"

Sean pulled her into his arms, holding her tight. "You know it wasn't. Damn it, Jules. I told you I have loved you since the first moment I heard you scream. That is all it took. One sound and I left everything behind without question. Something inside me broke the day I learned you'd left Southie. I wanted to come after you so many times, but I was scared I didn't deserve you. I had nothing to offer you when I first arrived."

Jules wrapped her arms around his neck. "I shouldn't have left without saying anything." She didn't have to specify she meant the first time. The look on his face said he knew what she was talking about. "I thought leaving would help clear my head, but I ended up running from the only person who could have seen me through it. You gave up an entire world to help me. So I promise you, if there is even the smallest chance your people might be here, we will find them. You helped me with my Earth problems. I will help you with your, ah, where are you from?"

"Qurilixen," he supplied.

"With your Qurilixen problem. If it takes the rest of our lives, we will find your people and your brother, and we'll help them however we can. Even if that means starting an intergalactic dating service. I'm sorry I didn't give us a chance, but I'm offering us one now—if you want it?"

Sean answered with a kiss, pressing his mouth fully to hers. Lips moved in subtle, sweet caresses and didn't stop even when he picked her up and carried her to his bedroom. His tongue slipped between her lips, persuading her mouth to open before pressing past the barrier of her teeth. He kept her close, but she didn't protest the tight embrace. She felt his desperation, and it matched her own. Jules wondered if it would always be like this between them.

They didn't bother to turn on the bedroom light,

and the soft glow from the hall caressed him in shadows. Sean made love to her slowly, taking his time to explore her body. They undressed each other, peeling back layers of clothes as if it were the first time. Heat washed over her flesh, bringing with it a tingling. Need erupted low in her belly. She ached to have him inside her, to feel the intimate contact that only joining could bring.

He made a light sound of pleasure, the moan eliciting one from her. The dragon glowed from within his gaze. When he looked at her, the unguarded expression penetrated deep, revealing all he felt for her—love, worry, hope, desire. His stomach rubbed along hers and his hips nestled. He urged her legs apart. Anticipation filled her, pooling in her thighs.

"You're amazing," he whispered, cupping a breast. "Part of me can't believe you're here with me."

Jules trembled, and her breathing hitched. The smell of his light cologne surrounded her. Warm lips enclosed a nipple, boldly nibbling the sensitive peak. He reached between her thighs, parting her slick folds. She squirmed for more, and he didn't disappoint. The firm heat of his erection replaced his fingers.

Sean rocked his hips, their bodies joining. His

hand stimulated her, intimately rubbing along her sex. Jules hooked a leg over his shoulder, letting the other one fall to the side. The position put pressure on all the right spots, and it didn't take long for the pleasure to build. He pushed up, bracing his arms as he increased his speed. Climax hit her hard, and she gasped her release. Her nails clawed his flesh, and she closed her eyes tight. Sean came with a jerk, groaning loud and long.

He fell to her side, instantly pulling her next to him. Her breath came in heavy pants. Heat radiated off them, but she didn't want to pull away even as sweat beaded along their flesh.

A small smile stretched across her face. She felt safe. Sean made her feel that way. She closed her eyes, wanting nothing more than this moment, resting in her lover's arms.

ALMOST ONE YEAR LATER...

"*After a trial lasting nearly seven months, East Boston's lady of crime, Juanita Velázquez, was sentenced to life without the possibility of parole thanks in part to the testimony of a local waitress and a Velázquez family bodyguard, Jose Guzman. Juanita is the sole survivor of the Velázquez crime family. Her brother Hector died the same day of her arrest, killed in an unrelated downtown shooting. It is expected that Ms. Velázquez's lawyers will file an appeal on her behalf. Prosecuting Attorney, Fredrick Myers, says his office is not concerned.*"

Jules lifted the remote, turning off the television as Myers's face appeared on the screen. She'd heard the man talk enough in the last several months that she didn't need to hear his sound bite on the news.

"It's over," she said for what had to be the thousandth time that day. Turning to Sean, she grinned. "It's finally over. I can't believe it."

"I was a little worried you'd be disappointed," he said. "All the excitement of a trial is dying down. The news cameras will go away to the next big thing."

"And that's a bad thing?" She chuckled, running her fingers over his cheek. A small growth of beard scratched her hand. "Honestly, they are cramping my style."

"Would you like me to get your woman's time medicine for the cramps?" He arched a brow. "I do not sense that it is time."

"One, stop sensing my periods," Jules answered. "Two, it is a saying. It means they're giant pains in the ass because they keep me from living life as I want."

"Ah, ass pain. I remember that saying. Ass pain and style cramping are the same thing. I understand." Sean nodded. "Now that it is over, I worry you will become bored with me and long for that next adventure."

"I'll have my adventure," Jules said. "I get to

make out with a dragon man. How many women get to say that and mean it?"

"If you say that, they will think you're crazy."

She shrugged. "Let them. So, did you think about what I found? Now that the trial is over, we can go to Louisiana like we talked about. That plantation hotel website boasts they have lizard man sightings in the bayou."

"I suppose it is worth looking into." He ran his finger down the tip of her nose.

"I know you're worried about leaving Southie in case your people come back here, but we won't be gone long. It has to be worth trying, doesn't it? If there is a chance this lizard man is a dragon-shifter, I know you can find him." She pressed her mouth gently to his. "And if it is a hoax, then we take a long deserved vacation to the swamps. No harm in looking."

"You're right. We'll go. But, I think you mainly want to travel to another planet to see what kind of trouble you can cause," he said. "I'm right, aren't I? You wish for another adventure to start."

"I can always join you in the bounty hunter business."

"You want to be a hunter?" Sean asked in surprise. He stroked his fingers through her hair. The blonde was completely gone, replaced by a darker shade. She'd colored it the second the trial was over.

"Hell, yes!" Jules grinned. "I want to be a bounty hunter. Jules Dalton, Bounty Hunter, has a nice ring to it. Brian already said he'd take me to get a gun, and Myrna said they have karate classes at the rec center."

Sean didn't move. For a second, she thought he might have stopped breathing.

"Unless…"

"Unless?" He jumped on the word almost desperately. His protective instincts hadn't let up. Sometimes she found them annoying. But mostly, she found it endearing.

"Unless you can offer me a better adventure, dragon man." Jules was only teasing him, but she couldn't help it. She felt giddy. The trial was over. Juanita was behind bars. Things were going well with Sean. He never asked her to marry him, but according to his people's tradition, they were mated and, according to Sean, that went much deeper than human vows. So much had changed in the last year. They were different. Better. Stronger.

"As a matter of fact, I can." He grinned as his eyes flashed with the threat of a shift. He leaped off the bed to go to the closet.

Hearing him rummage around, she asked, "You didn't buy some sort of toy, did you? Am I going to regret teaching you what the adult industry is?"

"Why?" came the garbled response. "Do we need more toys? Tired of me already?"

"You wish. Sorry, babes, you're stuck with me." Jules sat up, craning her neck to see what he was doing. The door blocked her view. When he came out empty-handed, she arched a brow. "Is it skydiving gear? Are you finally going to go with me?"

"No," came the expected response.

"But, I thought dragons liked to fly?" she pouted.

"I'm not that kind of dragon."

"Are you my surprise? I think I'm going to like this. You bought the cowboy outfit, didn't you?"

"Close your eyes and stop talking."

Jules giggled but followed his direction. Lying back on the bed, she waited for that first touch. Sean stroked her arm with a single finger. Her heart caught in her chest even as anticipation built.

Tracing her hand, he whispered, "This is the best adventure I have to offer you, Jules." Surprised by the catch in his voice, she opened her eyes to look at him. He gave her an endearing smile and shrugged. "What do you say?"

Jules followed his gaze down to her hand. She

hadn't felt him slip a ring onto her finger, but now a vintage style filigree white gold ring with a square shaped sapphire winked back at her in the lamplight.

"We have been mated according to the ways of my people. You are in every sense my wife by dragon-shifter tradition, but will you human mate to me?"

Seeing the symbol on her finger, she knew no moment had ever been so perfect. Slowly, she nodded, "Yes, Sean, this is the only adventure I'll ever need—being with you. Forever." Then, smiling, she added, "But if you think I'm giving up chasing bad guys to be a housewife you're sorely mistaken. When we get back from Louisiana, it's on. A few classes and I'll be ready to go full on ninja. In fact, I hear the North End has been having trouble with this punk named Joey Four Fingers—"

Sean stopped her words, pressing his mouth to hers in a deep kiss. When he pulled back, he said, "I think I like the bounty hunting idea better. Would you settle for being a partner, my sweet vigilante?"

Jules grabbed him and flipped him onto the bed, sliding her body on top of his to pin him down. She pulled at her shirt, tossing it aside to distract him with her breasts. It worked. His eyes instantly went to her chest. The heat from his body flowed over her thighs as she held down his arms. "Half the business will make a pretty kick-ass wedding present, but Joey's butt in a jail cell would be even better. I thought I could get a job undercover at his father's chop shop."

Sean growled, swinging his leg to dislodge her so he could roll on top. His hips flexed suggestively against her. "No wife of mine is chopping cars. You'll just have to settle for legally apprehending bail jumpers as a bounty hunter. How would that be?"

"Fine," she pretended to pout. Pulling his face to hers, she moaned softly at the willing acceptance of his mouth. When his hands stirred restlessly against her, and she had his mind clouded to logic with desire, she whispered, "I promise I won't chop the cars. I'll just be the receptionist."

The End

THE SERIES CONTINUES...
MISCHIEVOUS PRINCE

Captured by a Dragon-Shifter Book Five

*He's a dragon-shifting prince, and she's a human.
What could possibly go wrong?*

Dragon-shifter Prince Finn will do whatever it takes to save his people from extinction, even if that means sneaking through a portal to Earth to find a bride. With dragon men disappearing and threats to cut off their supply to eligible women, he knows the portal is their only hope of survival. And it might be his only chance to find love.

"First meets are easy. Staying is hard."

Food blogger, Sadie Harcourt isn't one for commitment. Her job offers the perfect excuse to keep moving. Never did she expect that her love of adventure would accidentally catapult her from Faulkner Alley in Oxford, Mississippi onto a planet of Alpha shifters looking to marry.

When the elders discover that Finn accessed the portal, all hell breaks loose. Factions pounce on the opportunity to overthrow the royal family. Now everything he holds dear rests in the hands of a captivating woman who arrived on his planet by mistake.

CHAPTER ONE EXTENDED EXCERPT

"Admit it, Ivar, you're intrigued." Prince Finn hoped his mischievous smile and lighthearted approach would convince his good friend to relax. Most cat-shifters were known for their untamed ways, but not Prince Ivar of the Var. If Finn hadn't known the man since childhood, he would have been intimidated by Ivar's frozen, stoic expression, and dead stare.

"This is highly irregular." Ivar folded his arms

over his chest. "We should not be meeting like this before the royal assembly with the elders."

Finn's expression fell. For a cat-shifter, the man was uptight and lacked any sense of adventure. He would have preferred Ivar's more carefree brother for this plan, but Rafe had married already and wouldn't be of any help. Ivar and Finn were the only unmated princes left on the planet.

The soft green-blue light of evening threw shadows over the valley. It wouldn't get too much darker. With three suns, the planet was cast in almost constant daylight. Finn liked the stillness of the valley, the gentle sway of the yellow-tinted grasses.

"I love our home world," Finn sighed in frustration. "I love my people. This is where I want to raise a family. I would do nothing to jeopardize any of this. And that is why I will fight for this place and my people."

Finn's words seemed to hang in the air. Ivar didn't move.

"Gods bones, Ivar," Finn swore, losing all pleasantry. "You know what will happen at that meeting—our parents and the elders will close the portal to Earth. They will demand it buried under a mountain so deep that no one will ever remember that it's there.

What do we tell our people in a hundred years? In three hundred? When our parents are gone, and they are looking at us to fix things as the last of shifter kind is dying out because the one viable option we had to find them wives was closed due to fear mongers and political maneuverings."

"Do you think their fears are unjustified? Already dragons have been sneaking through to Earth and not returning. You worry about the population? Yours is walking off this planet willingly. How many men have you lost to that portal? How many slip through and do not come back home? How many want to but can't come back, or don't know how? Each night it opens in a different location. We do not want to see our cat-shifter population dwindle over promises of a better life on Earth, promises you and I both know are exaggerated. Humans have not changed. You saw their films glorifying alien destruction. You have seen their taverns and their streets. They cannot even feed their own kind. People whisper that the portal leads to some great valley full of unmated woman waiting with open arms. We both know that is not the truth, but a false hope spread by opportunists."

"We opened the portals with the plan that we would show them it could work. All four of us would go through and find mates. Kyran and Rafe have succeeded. We at least have to try. If all four princes show a united front. If we prove to the people that Earth women will come if we do it correctly. If we—"

"I seem to remember you not being all that eager to marry the first night we went through," Ivar interrupted. "Or the several times after that. It was a game to you. You had your chance. You could have grabbed any number of women if that is what you wanted."

"I thought we'd have more time to decide. What is wrong in wanting to have a little fun first? Everyone says that when you see your mate you'll know. I've not felt anything concrete." Finn sighed. "I'm still waiting for the gods to speak to me. And I know you're waiting for them to speak to you. No man seeks a lonely life."

"I am not convinced the voices of our gods can be heard on Earth," Ivar stated. "There is too much noise, too much clutter."

"They spoke to our brothers." Finn took a deep breath and closed his eyes. He wasn't telling his friend the whole plan. He wouldn't. Not yet. Not until they were through the portal and on the other side. "Ivar, I'm asking you to come with me tonight. Let us prove this portal is a solution, not a problem."

Ivar's eyes turned toward the sky as if he contemplated the wide space beyond. "We have been building relations with alien cultures through our intergalactic contacts."

"Any that are compatible with shifters?" Finn questioned. The Draig did not like associating with space travelers. Often, the only reason aliens landed was because they wanted something—to steal resources, to sell their religions, or to take advantage of the locals.

"I'm not saying I don't think the portals could work, but..." Ivar's scowl deepened.

"What?"

Ivar lifted his chest. "I think they are mismanaged. If the portals were under Var guard, people would not be slipping through. They would be regulated."

"The valley entrance is locked. There are only a few keys. The palace entrance is guarded and reachable through a long tunnel." This was not the conversation Finn wanted to be having—a debate between royal families. "It could have been one of your guards, as easily as it was one of ours, that let the men through. That's what happens when you tell men you have the solution to their biggest problem but aren't ready to share it with them. Our parents and the elders are too busy arguing over the details, but nothing is being done. Now they want to close it because it's easier than dealing with it."

"You did not call me to this valley to argue." Ivar motioned to the cave. "I assume you want to go to Earth to look for brides?"

"Yes." Finn lifted two satchels from the ground. "I checked the charts and brought us supplies. We're going to," he paused, having to focus on the word to pronounce the foreign name, "*Miss-is-sip-pie.*"

"And you think that if I go with you to Miss Pie, and we both bring back the women ordained by the gods to be our wives, we can show up at that meeting and convince the elders and our parents to keep the portals open?"

"Yes. If they see that we are well matched."

"Why will this trip be any different from the others?"

"The gods will bless us. I know they will. We need this. Our people's future needs this."

"And if they don't?" Ivar cut straight to the point as always. "You know the odds are against us."

Finn stiffened and forced himself to meet Ivar's gaze. "Then we make them bless us."

Ivar arched a brow. "You want to lie about the

will of the gods? You would be willing to spend an eternity with a woman who was not your true mate?"

Finn nodded. "If it means the survival of the Draig, then yes, I will make that sacrifice. No one will ever know the truth beyond the two of us."

Ivar's mouth curled up at the side. It wasn't a smile so much as approval. The look took Finn by surprise since the man rarely showed approval of anything. "I did not think you had it in you to put our people before yourself. I misjudged you. Yes. I will go with you tonight to bring back brides so that we may ensure the future of our population. I will make this sacrifice with you. We will take half mates and never let a moment's unhappiness show. But I want something in return."

Finn was not delusional in believing that tonight would be special. Dropping the pretense of destined mates and love didn't make that knowledge any easier. "What?"

"Once we do this, we push for regulations for portal travel. We stop the flow of shifter defectors before the cats join the dragons. Staying on Earth cannot be an option."

Finn nodded. "Agreed. The Draig have discussed only going on the one night of Qurilixian darkness a year and making it a mass wedding celebration. It can become a ritual. We go, get brides, bring them back and celebrate those who are chosen. Men will have to be trained before they can go through the portal. It will become a rite of passage."

"One earned through honor," Ivar added.

"And in twenty years no one will question the tradition."

"I want Var access to the portal. We will build an embassy on Draig land, right here in the valley where both families will have a joint say over travel. My people need to know that we are not at the mercy of the dragons."

"And my people need to know the cats respect the fact that we have guarded these portals since our ancestors came here to escape Earth's tyranny. We took the risk by being the closest. If the human hunters ever found their way through, it was our people who would be the first in their path."

Ivar lifted his hand to take a satchel. "Then it is decided. Tonight, we enter through that portal to find brides by any means necessary."

Finn had never wanted his people to kidnap women. What if they didn't want to come? What if they were unhappy? What if he and Ivar never found peace in their marriages? They could be signing on for hundreds of years' worth of misery. Then again, what did the fate of four people mean when countered against the survival of thousands?

Updated Reading List and Links here:
MichellePillow.com

ABOUT MICHELLE M. PILLOW

New York Times & USA TODAY
Bestselling Author

Michelle loves to travel and try new things, whether it's a paranormal investigation of an old Vaudeville Theatre or climbing Mayan temples in Belize. She believes life is an adventure fueled by copious amounts of coffee.

Newly relocated to the American South, Michelle is involved in various film and documentary projects with her talented director husband. She is mom to a fantastic artist. And she's managed by a dog and cat who make sure she's meeting her deadlines.

For the most part she can be found wearing pajama pants and working in her office. There may or may not be dancing. It's all part of the creative process.

Come say hello! Michelle loves talking with readers on social media!

www.MichellePillow.com

facebook.com/AuthorMichellePillow

twitter.com/michellepillow

instagram.com/michellempillow

bookbub.com/authors/michelle-m-pillow

goodreads.com/Michelle_Pillow

amazon.com/author/michellepillow

youtube.com/michellepillow

pinterest.com/michellepillow

COMPLIMENTARY EXCERPTS

SPACE LORDS: HIS FROST
MAIDEN

A FREE EXTENDED SNEAK PEEK!

by Michelle M. Pillow

Empath and space pirate, Evan Cormier is obsessed with decoding an ominous premonition about his future. When a fellow crewman angered a spirit, the vengeful Zhang An took her wrath out on everyone in the vicinity. Evan just happened to be one of them. He's now facing a future in which he'll be forever alone.

Lady Josselyn of the House of Craven has been betrayed. With her home world on a Florencian moon under attack and her family dead, she finds herself at the mercy of the one who deceived them. There is only one thing left to do—die with honor. But before she can join her family in the afterlife, she must first avenge all that she held dear. Falling in love with a pirate was never in the plan. Evan and his thieving crewmates might have delayed her fate, but they can't stop destiny.

His Frost Maiden Excerpt

Craven Estates, Earth Settlement, Florencia's Fifth Moon

"Lift her," the General ordered, his shiny boots walking away from her, taking her reflection with it.

Two men hauled her to her feet, holding her up by her arms. Josselyn suppressed a cry as they jerked her dislocated shoulder. She couldn't see their faces, didn't need to. Her body hurt so badly she couldn't tell where the pain was coming from anymore.

The one who'd betrayed them stood before her. General Jack Stephans. He'd deceived her family and the fifth moon settlement. He'd traded them in for money and power. Josselyn lifted her gaze briefly to the hard depths of the steel green eyes before her. She wanted to kick, to give one last good blow, to go down fighting, but she couldn't raise her limbs.

"Poor little Josselyn, so heartbreaking," the

General grabbed her chin and swiped beneath her eye. He looked young, was in fact very young for his position, only a few years older than her six and twenty. And yet they all knew so much more of fighting than anyone their age should, than anyone ever should.

"We gave you a home," she whispered. "How could you do this? How could you join them?"

"You gave me a place in your stables," he spat, his grip tightening on her chin, bruisingly so. "Not a place at your table. Not a place by your side. Not equal. They gave me a rank, a title. They give me respect. They give me a place in this world."

"Jack," she said, her voice softening for the orphan boy they'd found over twenty years ago. If she begged him, maybe fate could be turned around; maybe this day could be erased. Fate had spit them out in a whirlwind of chance and deceit. Maybe all that had happened wasn't his fault. Maybe it wasn't hers. None of it mattered. None of it changed the fact that he had taken everything she held dear, everyone, and now he was robbing her of her family home. Her tone hardened and she closed her eyes. "General."

"Look at me, Josselyn," he said. His tone caught even as his grip on her face tightened until his fingers pressed the inside of her cheeks against her teeth. "You're so cold. Even now, your face is composed. Is one, lonely tear all the passion you can muster?"

"I am Lady Josselyn of the House of Craven." Her eyes opened slowly, focusing on the shiny white of his uniform. It gleamed with the orange glow coming from the fireplace. The material looked odd in the drabber earth tones many on the fifth moon wore. Theirs was a world based on Medieval Earth. Each moon in the Florencian system was different, each settlement patterned off a singular time in the human past, times that history had almost forgotten. But the principals of the ancestors who'd established the colonies no longer applied. Times were different now. What had started as preservation of history had turned into reality, into laws and a way of life they all believed in as generation after generation was raised into the worlds of the Florencian moons.

The General shook her by the face until finally she forced her eyes to meet his. He looked angry, hurt, wildly hopeful. "I can save you. I can say you had nothing to do with the treachery of your family. No one wants to kill a woman of noble blood. The line of Craven doesn't have to die. I will take your name; the name denied me by your father."

Was he serious? She knew he'd asked her father

for her hand in marriage. In fact, she'd dismissed the proposal with the full knowledge he only asked because he wanted power. Did he think she could love him now? Want him? Take him into her bed?

He must have read the answer on her face because his own expression hardened. She knew Jack. He wouldn't ask again.

"I suppose not," he said, almost sad. "Even if you agreed, I could never trust you not to take a blade to my back. Not after today." He sighed heavily. "Not after this."

"Ago," she whispered, even her voice beginning to fail in its strength, "pugna quod int-"

"Quiet your tongue! This house is mine. Mine." He let go of her chin and her head drooped. "And you can die knowing that I have taken more than what you all refused to give me in life."

"A place at our table," Josselyn said, her tone softer still, the will to live leaving her. Her heart called out to her ancestors, to her dead family, begging them to come and get her.

"My table," he answered, stepping away. The General lifted a gun, pointing it at her head. She heard the telltale click of metal on metal. The weapon was not one found on the fifth moon. They fought with swords and axes, like the old medieval ways. Though technology was available, not using it was a point of honor. He must have brought the weapon from another moon. Perhaps the Victorians? The Elizabethans? It appeared to be too old to be from much later in time.

"Do it, Jack." She didn't look at him as she waited for the final discharge of the gun, the loud bang before the end. When it didn't come, she repeated, the words a mere mouthing of her lips, "Do it."

"Speed you to a quick end, Josselyn Craven," Jack whispered. "You all brought this on yourselves."

To find out more about Michelle's books visit www.MichellePillow.com

Space Lords Series

His Frost Maiden
His Fire Maiden
His Metal Maiden
His Earth Maiden
His Woodland Maiden

LOVE POTIONS

BY MICHELLE M. PILLOW

Warlocks MacGregor® Book 1
Contemporary Paranormal Scottish Warlocks

A little magickal mischief never hurt anyone...

Erik MacGregor, from a clan of ancient Scottish warlocks, isn't looking for love. After centuries, it's not even a consideration...until he moves in next door to Lydia Barratt. It's clear that the shy beauty wants nothing to do with him, but he's drawn to her nonetheless and determined to win her over.

Lydia Barratt just wants to be left alone to grow flowers and make lotions in her old Victorian house. The last thing she needs is a demanding Scottish man meddling in her private life. Just because he's gorgeous and totally rocks a kilt doesn't mean she's going to fall for his seductive manner.

But Erik won't give up and just as Lydia let's her guard down, his sister decides to get involved. Her little love potion prank goes terribly wrong, making Lydia the target of his sudden embarrassingly obsessive behavior. They'll have to find a way to pull Erik out of the spell fast when it becomes clear that Lydia has more than a lovesick warlock to worry about. Evil lurks within the shadows and it plans to use Lydia, alive or dead, to take out Erik and his clan for good.

Love Potions Excerpt

"Ly-di-ah! I sit beneath your window, laaaass, singing 'cause I loooove your a—""

"For the love of St. Francis of Assisi, someone call a vet. There is an injured animal screaming in pain outside," Charlotte interrupted the flow of music in ill-humor.

Lydia lifted her forehead from the kitchen table. Her windows and doors were all locked, and yet Erik's endlessly verbose singing penetrated the barrier of glass and wood with ease.

Charlotte held her head and blinked heavily. Her red-rimmed eyes were filled with the all too poignant look of a hangover. She took a seat at the table and laid her head down. Her moan sounded something like, "I'm never moving again."

"You need fluids," Lydia prescribed, getting up to pour unsweetened herbal tea from the pitcher in the fridge. She'd mixed it especially for her friend. It was Gramma Annabelle's hangover recipe of willow bark, peppermint, carrot, and ginger. The old lady always had a fresh supply of it in the house while she was alive. Apparently, being a natural witch also meant in partaking in natural liquors. Annabelle had kept a steady supply of moonshine stashed in the basement. If the concert didn't stop soon she might try to find an old bottle.

"*Ly-di-ah!*"

"Omigod. Kill me," Charlotte moaned. "No. Kill him. Then kill me."

"*Ly-di-ah!*"

Erik had been singing for over an hour. At first, he'd tried to come inside. She'd not invited him and the barrier spell sent him sprawling back into the yard. He didn't seem to mind as he found a seat on some landscaping timbers and began his serenade. The last time she'd asked him to be quiet, he'd gotten louder and overly enthusiastic. In fact, she'd been too scared to pull back the curtains for a clearer look, but she was pretty sure he'd been dancing on her lawn, shaking his kilt.

"Omigod," Charlotte muttered, pushing up and angrily going to a window. Then grimacing, she said, "Is he wearing a tux jacket with his kilt?"

"Don't let him see you," Lydia cried out in a panic. It was too late. The song began with renewed force.

"He's..." Charlotte frowned. "I think it's dancing."

Since the damage was done, Lydia joined Charlotte at the window. Erik grinned. He lifted his arms to the side and kicked his legs, bouncing around the yard like a kid on too much sugar. "Maybe it's a traditional Scottish dance?"

Both women tilted their heads in unison as his kilt kicked up to show his perfectly formed ass.

"He's not wearing..." Charlotte began.

"I know. He doesn't," Lydia answered. Damn, the man had a fine body. Too bad Malina's trick had turned him insane.

**To find out more about Michelle's books
visit www.MichellePillow.com**

PLEASE LEAVE A REVIEW

Please take a moment to share your thoughts by leaving a review. Thank you for reading!

Be sure to check out Michelle's other titles at www.michellepillow.com

www.ingramcontent.com/pod-product-compliance
Lightning Source LLC
Chambersburg PA
CBHW030618120726

47904CB00006B/1947